Colder Greyer
Stones

Colder Greyer Stones

Tanith Lee

NewCon Press
England

First edition, published in the UK November 2013
by NewCon Press

NCP65 paperback

10 9 8 7 6 5 4 3 2 1

Cover art by John Kaiine
Cover design by Andy Bigwood

Minimal editorial interference by Ian Whates
Text layout by Storm Constantine

Contents

1. Introduction   7
2. Clockatrice   9
3. Malicious Springs   33
4. The Greyve   53
5. The Heart of Ice   67
6. Calinnen   85
7. En Forêt Noire   93
8. Fr'eulogy   113
9. The God Orkrem   117
10. In the Country of the Blind   129
11. My Heart: A Stone   131
12. Killing Her   165
13. The Frost Watcher   171
14. About the Author   207

Break, break, break,
On thy cold gray stones, O Sea!
And I would that my tongue could utter
The thoughts that arise in me.

Break, Break, Break,
Tennyson

Cold Grey Stones Revisited

An Introduction

Ian Whates

I first discovered Tanith Lee's writing while on holiday in Spain. As ever, I had underestimated how much reading I would do in two weeks and, with several days' holiday still remaining, had finished all the books I'd brought with me. The local shops offered very little by way of science fiction and fantasy, but I picked up two cooks whose covers caught my eye. These were *The Book of the Damned* and *The Book of the Beast*, both by Tanith Lee; an author I'd heard much about but had never actually read.

This proved to be one of the wisest impulse buys I've ever made. Within the first few pages of *The Book of the Damned* I was completely hooked; on the characters, on the setting – Paradys, surely the most vividly realised city since Fritz Leiber's Lankhmar – but most of all on the writing.

Through her careful choice of words and expert sculpting of phrases, the author managed to bring the narrative to life. I could *feel* the horror, *feel* the lust, *feel* the torment of the characters whose lot was laid bare within these pages; I could taste the decadence and magic that permeated every brick and stone of this ancient, gothic city.

I became totally immersed, and emerged at the books' conclusion blinking up at the daylight and questioning whether the world I returned to was any more real than the one I'd left behind between the covers of these Secret Books of Paradys. Tanith's writing does that; seduces you and transports you to realms of her imagining.

In January 2012, I was privileged enough to launch NewCon Press' new *Imaginings* series with *Cold Grey Stones,* a volume of fiction from Tanith Lee: eleven wonderful and rich-textured stories, all previously uncollected, five of which appeared for the first time anywhere and all of which deserved to be treasured. Available only as a signed limited edition hardback, *Cold Grey Stones* sold out in a matter of weeks, and I could have sold the print run twice over.

Tanith had originally intended to write one further new story for the book: "The Frost Watcher", a tale inspired by her husband John's fabulous cover art. In the event, for a variety of reasons, "The Frost Watcher" failed to be either completed or included. Tanith and I have always regretted that the stories in *Cold Grey Stones* never reached a wider audience… And in the interim, of course, "The Frost Watcher" has been written. It seems foolish to publish this extraordinary novelette anywhere other than beneath the cover that inspired it. So, we have taken the decision to issue *Colder Greyer Stones,* a paperback only collection containing all the stories in the original book but with the content expanded to accommodate this wonderful new tale, which finally appears where it was always intended to.

The fact that the book's release coincides with Tanith being honoured at World Fantasy Convention 2013 with a 'Lifetime Achievement Award' only makes the appearance of the expanded and retitled *Colder Greyer Stones* all the more appropriate.

Ian Whates
November 2011 / August 2013

Clockatrice

Dare I say, like the genius composer Shostakovich, I'm fascinated by clocks — be they working or retired. One day I bought a medium-size clock, lacking all insides, (it has since received an effective face and hands) and clothed in thin slabs of green onyx, with little gilded feet that peculiarly resemble birds with upraised wings. My husband (John Kaiine) called it the Clockatrice. And my mind at once began to work out how that deadly creature, the cockatrice, which turns any viewer into stone, might be connected to a clock. The result of my mental game follows.

I

Poor girl. Beautiful Diana, named for a goddess, and barely sixteen years of age. Just after midnight she descended through the gardens to meet her lover. And before any clock could strike one, she was as beautiful as she was dead.

The gardens at Sessonby are still very fine, but back then, in the 1590s, they had a reputation, being influenced by startling new discoveries, and even alchemy. Mazes of topiary cut in extraordinary forms (swans, minotaurs), looping paths that led to groves dominated by such items as gigantic bronze astrolabes. These indicated the place was full of magical clues. They were clever gardens, where also nocturnally sometimes hares appeared, spirit-like, from the park outside, wolfish foxes, or snakes with enamelled skins — creatures of sorcery and impulse. The Queen herself, the Great She, Elizabeth, had visited Sessonby.

Diana had no thought for the Queen, even though Diana's hair was hennaed to amber, fashionably, to honour the Queen's own tresses, (or, by now, her wigs.)

The moon however, Queen of Night, did exercise some authority. Full this evening, it hunted things as it moved westward, striking between screens and curtains of leaves. A stone satyr, for example, with sly, sidelong eyes, or an owl of marble that seemed to alight on spread wings below the steps. And Diana, too. For whenever it could, the moon splashed her with illumination, her blonde yellow dress with its shield-stiff bodice, the tops of her tender breasts above, her white face, and her hands flitting to the narrow gate.

Outside the gate opened a glade. This was of course contrived, and at its centre stood a shadow clock, based on an artefact of the ancient Egyptians, as perhaps authorized by Elizabeth's own Magus, John Dee. The way the sun fell on the clock would tell the hours. But at noon the clock's position must be reversed in order to monitor the hours after. Tonight the clock looked spitefully alert. Instead of daylight the moon boiled white across its brazen spike. And beyond loomed the huge pine trees, which Diana's great grandfather had planted in the time of Henry VII, the Tudors' first bloody-handed king.

It was said a stag had been killed on the spot and buried whole there, the tree then planted in its vitals. Nourished by the feast the pine grew to vast height and girth.

Diana had never liked the pine, and maybe this story was the cause. She had had an old nurse as well in childhood, who said the pine was unnatural and ate any small animals that strayed near it. Even a little child, once.

A tremendous silence had filled the gardens. Diana noticed that especially now she herself had ceased to move. Quite often, inflamed by a full moon, a bird might sit singing. (Just as moths were stirred up, and fluttered about.) Tonight no bird sang. Not a thread of wind silked the branches. The foreign shrubs had congealed to black linen and gave off no perfume.

Why had she made a promise to meet her lover here? They had slight need to be hasty, or furtive, she and Robert, for they were betrothed and soon to be wed. Some fancy of his, and she had acquiesced, as a wife must learn to do. But see, he had failed her, had not bothered to arrive after all. She should return at once to the house.

The moon slipped a notch along the sky, and a single ray shot between the leaves like a white spear.

A curious odour was on the air. It suggested – chickens, Diana thought, yet too something tindery, corrosive, and old.

And then she did hear a sound, which was not the wind through the leaves, nor the rustle of her dress. It was high above her.

Unwillingly she lifted her gaze, up, up the length of the pine tree, among its bristled knots of needles. What did she see? Something? Only a black shadow, shifting and turning, and then the moon's relentless ray slithered on a length of substance almost like chainmail, the half-metallic armour of a serpent or a lizard.

Astonished, Diana stared. She could make nothing of it, and yet her heart beat with tremendous blows. She wished immediately to run away. But the noise came once more, that strange thin hissing, and the faint stink on the air blew over her, through her, and she could not move. She could not lift one foot from the ground, not even one hand to cover her eyes that would not close. Then silence fell back into the garden. It filled her up. It drowned her from within. Her heart had frozen. Diana was a thing of petrified material. She was colourless, amber and blonde all gone away, gray like the satyr, moon-like as the marble owl. She had been changed to stone, and as stone they found her the next day, in the glade below the pine tree. Where you may see her still. Tonight even, if you wish.

"Certainly there's a statue there of a young girl," he said, "in authentic Elizabethan clothes. Obviously tourists get told the story of what happened, and how she was turned to granite."

"Do they believe it?"

"Do you?"

"Yes."

"Christ," he said, and laughed.

"Christ," she answered briskly, "could of course undo any evil spell and set her free. Are you expecting Him to visit?"

Robert Trenchall frowned at her. He had a strong, dark face and the sort of brooding eyes she had seen already in pictures of him in various magazines. His black hair was attractively long, hanging just over the collar of his leather jacket.

Probably she should resist the urge to challenge him. He could always have her thrown off his property. She was not even a journalist, only a freelance photographer.

"Last night," Dru continued, now she hoped in a calm, pacifying way, "you said we could see the statue."

"I did. But no one took me up on it."

She thought he must hate it all, allowing people to traipse about the gardens and the rest of the estate of Sessonby. His aunt, the late, famous artist, Vera Reive, had left it to him, with all its debts, five years before. He was seldom here save in the line of duty, which must drag him away from his other work in the theatre, and with music. Dru recalled an interview in which he said he would have loved Sessonby, had it not been for the constant need to prostitute the place, (tours, weekends, Historical Nights) in order to secure its upkeep.

The previous evening had been part of just such a junket. An expensive, lavish dinner in the grand dining room, and the appropriate music and story-telling by Trenchall and a pair of his actor friends. The last tale, dramatically relayed just after midnight, was the legend of poor Diana Sesby, who in 1594 became literally petrified by the breath of a cockatrice, hatched in the pine tree at the foot of the gardens. Indeed, no one had taken up Trenchall's offer of viewing the stony corpse. Possibly his scowl had deterred them. Or the pouring English rain.

But it was 10 a.m. now, and full light of a May morning.

"So where," she said, "should I go?" Then realizing, she

added sweetly, "aside, obviously, from hell?"

"Sorry," he said, scowling now at his combat boots, firmly embedded in early summer mud.

"That's OK. It must be – difficult. But I am interested."

"I'll take you there," he said.

"There's no –"

"It's fine. The way the gardens are now, you might get lost. No, I don't mean because you're some dumb damn stupid woman. The mazes are overgrown, and the steps, of course, partly gave way years back. Just bear with me, and I'll guide you down."

Dru glanced at him. Her guide into the dark. For even at this pre-noon hour, she had already seen the world of the gardens below was steeped in shadow, sombre and unsure.

"Thanks," she said. And went with him along the swampy lawn.

Diana Sesby still stood in the tangled glade. The pine tree was still there too, towering up, no doubt grown taller since the sixteenth century.

The whole space was determinedly blank, despite the bright sunlight. It might have been roofed by a dome of polarized glass.

Dru edged around the statue. It was the only one, the satyr and the owl were missing, as was the mysterious shadow clock. She could not be sure the remaining sculpture was genuinely Elizabethan, but the carven garments looked authentic, the stiff bodice and ornately arranged hair. Even the long string of – presumably – pearls. One omission though, no ruff behind the neck. Which was a little odd. Ruffs had been a fashion must in the 1590s.

Dru had thought Trenchall would leave her once he had shown her how to negotiate the steps. But no, he was loitering, watching.

Raising the Olympus, she aimed and took a slanting shot of the petrified girl.

"Not digital, then?" Trenchall remarked.

"No." She framed another lower shot. Straightening, she said, "One puzzle. If something turns you to stone, why do your clothes turn too? I mean, flesh and blood and bone and hair – fine. That's living matter, or only recently dead, like hair-ends and nails. But a dress? A necklace… I'm no scientist, but that makes no sense to me. Never has."

"Hey, maybe it didn't happen, then. Maybe she's only a statue."

"Except…" said Dru. She leaned forward and peered into the statue's face. Diana Sesby, if it was she, had been a good seven inches shorter. Which made it easier to stare down and to see – "My God," Dru said. He did not respond. "I assume other people have noticed this, er, detail?"

"Yes."

Dru, however, realigned the camera for a close-up. He had the courtesy to keep quiet as she angled in on the tiny moth, caught there just above the girl's stone temple, at the edge of her immutable hairline. The moth was also formed of stone, and chiselled with an incredible, one might say a needless, delicate accuracy. The wings were thin enough to be translucent. Two minuscule antennae were just visible against the tendrils of human hair.

Trenchall said, "And yes, it resembles the proper sort of moth for the time. And yes, it seems to be part of the statue, matching stone, etc. But I wouldn't bet on its credentials. A cunning fake is much more likely."

Sunday evening was to be the banquet in the old hall, under the rafters in "a shining forest of candles," as the brochure put it. It was the climax of the weekend, but Dru missed it. The reason being that she was instead up in Robert Trenchall's private rooms.

His invitation had arrived about an hour before the official meal was due to start. One of the house gofers brought it, smiling and non-committal.

Dru wondered if Trenchall frequently chose a single young woman from the medley of guests. And if he did, was it a perk for him or a prize for her? She could politely refuse. But she had always quite fancied him. She liked his music enough too. Besides, she was curious. Even if they did not end up in the sack, she had no objections to seeing some of the house that lay off the public route.

In fact, his flat, as he called it, was very plain and very much modernized, with pale walls and darkly pale curtaining, and only contemporary abstract pictures that, while Dru thought them quite good, were not to her taste. Outside the high windows the gardens shaded rapidly under more threatening clouds. A necessary wood fire had been lit in the main room, un-Elizabethan but warming.

Trenchall greeted her with easy grace, as if they had known each other some while, and theirs was a liaison of mutual if light-hearted respect. They ate smoked salmon, steaks, strawberries, and drank a French white wine sturdy enough to cope with pink fish, red meat, and scarlet fruit.

"I'm glad you like the wine," he said. "I thought you would. I chose it with you in mind."

"Really. How thoughtful."

He grinned. Oh, irresistible. "I imagine," he said, "you'll be working this up, I mean the tour here, into something you can sell."

"No," Dru said. "I can't afford to pay estate fees for using any of the Sessonby legends professionally. Let alone pictures from the grounds. It was just personal interest."

"In other words, you'll devise something different enough, then rip us off."

Dru looked at him cautiously. It had all been going so well. "I don't do that, Mr. Trenchall."

"Robert. Of course you do it. Any artist, photographer, writer who comes here does it. I do it whenever I go anywhere –

I use anything that interests me. And if I can't afford to pay, I change it so it's something more – how shall I say? – original."

Dru put down her glass. "If you like, I'll sign a disclaimer."

"Listen, Dru, I really don't mind. I don't care." He sat back. "Tell me, what do you really think of Diana's statue? The whole rigmarole?"

"I think it could be true," she said flatly. "Why not? Peculiar stuff happens all the time. Yes, it will probably have a rational explanation, or at least a scientifically provable one. But it can still happen. Imagine if someone had told a man in Shakespeare's time that every snowflake has an intricate and unique pattern. Very likely, in those days, he would believe you. And it's a fact. But when someone told you that the first time – weren't you astounded?"

"I don't recall. Maybe."

"You should have been. It's crazy."

"The cockatrice though," he said. He paused, then said, "When I was a kid Vera – aunt Vera Reive – scared the shit out of me with that story. The egg – they get born from eggs, it seems, like snakes and other reptiles – was centuries old, caught up somehow in the young stem of the pine tree. As the tree grew, so did the egg. They matured together. And of course, it had been nourished with blood. They originate in the Middle East, or the Med – depends who you read – cockatrices. Or -trixes, whatever the plural is. A cock-bird with the back end and tail of a lizard. Somehow that is such a disgusting idea. Not like a man with a bull's head or a girl with the tail of a fish – they seem OK, aesthetically, if you like... But that combination. Chicken flesh and reptile. I had bad dreams for a year."

"You never used it in your music, did you?"

"Fuck no. Wouldn't want to. But think of it. Just think of it." He sat forward and suddenly gripped her hand across the table. A curious seduction move? Or did he mean all this? His handsome face was intense and serious. "It hatched that very night, when that poor bloody girl, Diana – a kid, just sixteen –

came down to meet her faithless lover. And its poisonous chicken-lizard breath turned her to stone, that's how they do it, it seems, and the moth caught in her hair and went to stone too. But she was just as stricken, as helpless, as a moth."

"Why did her clothing change to stone too?" Dru asked again, a sharp stab at practicality.

But he smiled then, still holding her hand. "You're a hard lady, hard as stone. Let me tell you then. It didn't. The statue was naked. That's the actual story. The stone garments, even the stone pearls, were carved and added later. Her original ones were in ribbons, some on the ground, all torn and shredded, as if a "Hurricano" had blown them off. And the ruff was so fragile it had disintegrated completely into nothing. They never tried to replace it in stone, thought it extra unlucky. They'd brought in John Dee, apparently, the Queen's alchemist. But by then the cockatrice was gone. Flown away. It had chicken wings, obviously. Or is it bat-wings? It could do what it bloody well wanted."

Her hand was still in his. She said, "I like the story. Why didn't you tell this part last night, to the others?"

"The others were pissed and thick as four short planks. And you don't like the story. It makes your flesh creep. And you believe. As I do. Even though I don't. Naturally."

"Yes."

Then he rose and leaned across the table and kissed her. Dru enjoyed the kiss. She had thought she would.

"I'll tell you about the clock," he said. "But in a little while."

They slow-motioned into the bedroom. A masculine yet comfortable room, and this time with central heating. The sex was very, very good.

Next morning, (Monday) standing with the other visitors, at 11 a.m., her bag on the drive, waiting for the communal coach, she saw a taxi drive up.

A thin, chic American girl got out, very blonde and with

flawless teeth, which she did not reveal until Robert Trenchall appeared. "Hi Robbie!"

"Hi, Zuzi," said Robert Trenchall.

Neither of them now saw anyone else in the whole world. Even a gofer had to come out to pay the cab. She had predicted nothing else, not since rising at seven, when Trenchall had kissed her quickly on the cheek and said, "Apologies, but we have to hurry. My steady's due back any minute."

Steady. What a nice, old-fashioned term.

Dru had been out of his flat inside five minutes.

And by sunset, she was back in London.

II

Lucky boy. Gallant Robert Southurst, named for his father and eighteen years of age. That night in 1594, he had been with his low-life mistress, who held him yet in a grasp of greed and menace, and thus he failed to meet Diana in the gardens at Sessonby. As she was struck to stone, he was howling with the pleasures of lust, and so escaped a fate similar to hers.

Sometime after, when Robert Southurst had seemingly recovered from the remorse and revulsion occasioned by his bride-to-be's end, (and its type) he was persuaded to marry another. Diana had been youthful and lovely, and he had liked her well enough. The new wife was two or three years Robert's elder, of the sternest Protestant leaning, and a shrew. He managed to sire four children on her, or somebody did. But a vox populi of the time reports that, in his thirties, he declared, "My true bride was slain by a cucu-trix. While I, alas, have wed it!"

He did outlive this spouse nevertheless. And in his fortieth year devised a number of curious mechanical toys. These were put together by various artisans, and paraded about his own house, (Longhampton) to the fascination and fright of callers.

The most elaborate of the inventions was, so contemporary chroniclers had it, a "Grete Clocke" that had been established in one of the west chambers.

This artefact, reportedly seven feet in height and trimmed with ebony, gold, and silver, kept good time all day and evening, until it sounded the fateful twelve of midnight. On the twelfth stroke, a pallid figure would glide out from a panel set in below the clock-face, a figure almost life-size, which represented a slender young girl with blonde-orange hair and a blonde gown. Though a doll, she closely resembled, it appeared, Diana Sesby. Enough so that an old woman who had known Diana, on seeing the apparition, fainted, and died not long after.

Having left the clock, the figure (stiffly, one must suppose) turned its head once to either side, then lifted its arms as if in supplication. But then they fell, and the animation slid slowly – and "moste fearsomely" – back into the clock-case. Following which the panel closed, and the clock ceased its motion with a clank. In order that it resume full function the next day, it must be wound up, and such was its ponderous quality, several men were needed for the task. None liked it, either. They had been known to say the clock was cursed, and would cast all Longhampton into the Pit.

Notably, aside from the unnerving Diana doll, the base of the clock rested on two bizarre supports. They were described as two "Crowing Cocks" of blackest basalt, each about four feet high, and with gilded beaks, claws and crests, and the raised wings of "Gryphones." They stood savagely erect on their hugely taloned feet, in attitudes suggesting extreme rage and violence. While from the rear of both swelled out a lizard's backside, ending in a horrid coiled tail, these endpieces of contrastingly purest white-silver, scored to an armoury of scales.

They had been heard to hiss too, the pair of creatures. They did it randomly, if always between sunfall and dawn. One maidservant of the house had gone mad, her hair turning white and falling from her head in a single night, because, as she swore on the holy name of the Christ, both beasts one dusk had turned to glare at her, their ruby eyes giving off a tinderous flash. The west chamber was said to have stunk for several hours, a reek like a poultry-yard, but also of gunpowder.

It was not generally an age of long life, but Robert Southurst survived both the death of the Queen, and the eras of King James and the primary Charles, Robert himself leaving the world in his seventy-first year. He had by then also survived two further wives, but he had kept them busy. He had peopled his house all told with seven sons and nine living daughters.

About three nights before that of his demise, Robert was sitting banked up on pillows in his bed – the custom then, rather than lie flat.

He was an old man, of course, his near seventy-one more the equivalent of a modern eighty-six. His lush black hair was all gone and he wore a night-cap. He was drinking one too, mulled wine from the fire now sinking on the bedroom hearth.

Outside the insectile, many-paned eyes of the windows, a thin tired moon was lying on the black sky. It was a cold midnight, at autumn's end.

Robert believed himself awake. But then a panel opened in the tapestried wall, and out glided a slender young woman with hennaed hair. And her gown was all in rags and streamers, and through it he glimpsed her fair white body, more glimpses than she had ever allowed him during their courtship. For he knew her at once as Diana Sesby.

"God's mercy," whispered Robert, and spilled his wine down the embroidered coverlet.

But Diana said to him plaintively, "Oh, Robert, my dear love, why did you not come to meet me that night?"

And he shook from head to toe in the warm bed, and his feet went cold as frost.

"Which night? When – when?"

"That night you bade me seek for you in the glade below my

father's garden. The glade with the pine tree growing there."

"Did I not meet you, surely I did, my lovesome Diana," he said, not able to help himself, frozen with terror and yet racked with pity.

"No, you were not there. Instead the Devil came and opened his bony serpent wings in the tree. His scaled tail coiled all around the branches, just as we are told it did in Eden. Oh, Robert, I wish I had seen you before he shut me fast in stone. But all I saw was the red back of his throat, like the stenchy gape of Hell, and now I am stopped forever, and all forevers that may be."

"Poor girl," said the old man in the bed, and wept.

But she only turned her head, once to the left, once to the right, then raised her arms in supplication, and let her arms fall down again by her sides. Just as the doll did that came out of the clock. Yet instead of sliding away backwards into the wall as the doll had into the clock-case, Diana Sesby merely vanished.

"I have dreamed," said Robert. "I have dreamed and now I am awake again." But he knew he had not dreamed, and that he had not slept. "It is to be my death," he said. And he was quite correct.

A single text remained that described the anecdote. Because the priest that secretly heard the pre-mortis confession of Robert Southurst, (who clandestinely had remained a Catholic all those years) was so troubled by it, he committed this section to paper.

But in Cromwell's time, less than a decade later, the chapel where the priest's books were kept was burned, along with a great many other things. And so, by now, no record exists.

To herself, Dru admitted that Trenchall had annoyed her. Not, obviously, by not wanting to prolong their sexual adventure, (she herself had neither anticipated nor wanted that) but by his truly bloody awful bad manners. Which had been equally evidenced in his underhanded treatment of the presumably unaware blonde

American.

Dru's annoyance was perhaps surprisingly sharp for a few days. And once she sloughed it, she decided she would after all make something creative of her weekend at Sessonby.

Having had her photographs printed by the usual team, she studied each shot. There was one particular take of the Diana statue, more luck, she felt, than expertise – for the glade had been so dark and the ground so sludgy, (and he, a distraction). The picture showed the entire statue, all four foot nine of her, from sweeping skirt-hem to just above the top of her head. And the clearest of detail was in it, everything side-lit in a quite un-clichéd way. Even the tiny moth was totally visible in the largest A3 print.

Aside from this Dru had retained, and written up, the other story, which Trenchall had told her during their night. It was, he said, a "Family Myth."

The notional clock intrigued Dru very much. She accordingly spent another handful of days trying to locate references to it, both via the computer, and in an estimable London library. But despite plenty of data on the house and grounds of Longhampton, (most of which, structure and park, had unfortunately burned to the ground in 1706) no mention of any unusual horology was on offer.

Doubtless the whole scenario of the clock was an invention, including the guilty-conscience figure of Diana which emerged from it. Although Dru believed in miracles and wonders, she had not often discovered one that would stand up to proper scrutiny.

That in mind, and neither the Longhampton nor the Sessonby searches yielding anything on the clock, (let alone Trenchall having spoken to any of the other weekend guests about it) he might have made the "Myth" up solely for her benefit. It was fair game then for a steal. After all, he had assured her he did not care if she utilized Sessonby history and folklore. And they had paid each other in kind, had they not? Accounts settled. They were quits.

Her plan was to employ one large piece of computer art, which would use the statue, rather altered, and two smaller pictures, mostly artistically invented. These she would link with a thousand words of unornamented prose, the entirety presented as a sort of anonymous horror tale of 16th Century England.

A heavily illustrated and well-paying US magazine, for which Dru had worked before on specific assignments, seemed very interested when she approached them. It would need, she thought, the rest of the month to put everything together.

What required the lengthiest labor, naturally, was the mock-up of the clock.

It had to look completely solid and three-dimensional, and though it would be feasible to enhance the impression through Photoshop, for maximum effect the more real the object was to start with the better. Diana, or her statue, was after all solid and real. And even when changed – no longer stone, her hair a deep russet red, (more like Elizabeth I's later wigs) and her dress the color of a hot chestnut, plus gold chains dangling round her neck and chest rather than pearls – even the moth translated into a night-flying horned beetle – she should, hopefully, look startlingly alive. The effect Dru was aiming for was a still from an intelligent, theatrical, and beautifully-lit movie.

Jack, a guy she knew from way back, helped Dru assemble the clock, along with his usual assistant, Pete. The clock's ingredients were many and various, including sheet metal, salvage, tin foil, fake gold-leaf, and not disdaining papier mache.

"It won't stand much knocking about, this won't," said Jack, proud but dubious.

"I'll take very good care of it," Dru promised. "I'm just going to light it, and then take its picture about nine trillion times."

Her studio flat near Camden was exactly that, a studio. A tiny bedroom lay behind a plasterboard wall, next to a bathroom the size of a cupboard. The kitchen area was generally only active with the making of tea, coffee and juice, occasional storage of wine and beer, and an insane toaster that tended to throw the cooked toast straight at the ceiling.

By the hour of the clock's glorious completion, the whole flat reeked of paints and adhesives. Fortunately these substances never affected Dru. And Pete, high as a kite, did not mind at all.

Dru did the shoot. This went very well. And when the prints came back, she could see what she thought to be a winner.

The other two smaller studies were shaping up pretty well also. As for the text, it only needed to sound neat and cool – cool in both senses. Heartless, preferably.

She had not really thought of Robert Trenchall while she worked. The young Elizabethan man in her revised narrative did not have the name of Robert either. Dru had changed all the names. Diana, in Dru's version, was named Susan. While Robert Southurst received the evocative title of Francis Rustember. A wonderfully improbable and untraceable invention.

The package was delivered to the editor in New York by the second week in June. London meanwhile blazed up in one of its normally brief heat-waves, which would likely finish in icy rain or hailstorms.

Dru's piece was accepted inside another week. Substantially altered by her from the Trenchall tale. Dru had the young, not-betrothed-but-wife hurrying alone to meet her husband in a deep forest, having been led to think him in deadly danger. But the villainous Francis Rustember, wanting rid of her, had sent her there instead to meet with a pair of hired murderers. The cockatrice, or cocatrix as Dru's fiction had it, (Old French-English via Latin) was roused by the aura of terror and sadism, and transmuted both the assassins and the hapless young wife to stone. Francis next had the clock made, with all its cockatrice imagery – less from guilt than as a spurious memorial, which placed any blame upon an uncanny monster, and so further obscured Francis's own monstrousness. One night however, the shade of Susan Rustember stepped from the clock to accuse him. Nor did she, in Dru's take, emerge from any handy panel or tapestry, but out of a whirling vortex where the face of the clock had been – the face of time itself. Susan-Diana informed Francis-Robert that, though physically immobilized, the vehicle of the time-piece had both imbued her with the nature of the cockatrice, and conveyed her phantom forward through the years. "Your heart," she said, "is already like a stone. So be it, then." And fixed her husband-now-widower with flaring crimson eyes like fire. Francis Rustember was found the next morning, dead but with no visible mark. Yet when his attendants tried to lift the corpse, its weight was so colossal, and all out of proportion to his girth, that a physician was called, (perhaps John Dee?) and opened up the body. At which they discovered, there in the chest cavity, Rustember's heart petrified to a solid mass of granite.

III

The mini heat-wave died next day. Rain hosed London down like an elementally deranged fire-fighter.

Dru's open windows were quickly shut. A plan to go to a party she was not that keen on was shelved. She ate a ham sandwich and an apple, and drank a pot of tea, showered, and went to bed with Joseph R. Concorde's *The Photographer's Bible: 1920-1975*.

Perhaps an hour after going to sleep, Dru woke again. (She was never certain of the precise time. Her bedside clock had stopped, also the bigger wall-clock in the outer room.) Her first impression was that the noise of the rain, hitting on all the windows, had increased and disturbed her.

Dru lay on her back, listening intently. No. The noise she heard was not rain. The night, aside from a faint London snore of traffic, was very still. What then was that shuffling, scratching sound? A rat? A year before one had got into the roof-space, but been evicted before it caused problems. This now did have a resemblance to that ratty tumbling skitter Dru recalled. But if it were a rat, this rat must be at least twenty times the original's size. And – not alone. Definitely the sounds were slightly out of synch, duplicated. Everything came twice.

Sitting up, Dru learned she was cold with fear. A fear out of all proportion to anything she had so far detected, let alone thought of. Her fear was way ahead of her.

And then. She heard the hissing.

So many things might hiss – a leaky valve, a damaged oxygen cylinder – she knew those. A cat might hiss, a snake, these too… And dragons, of course, hissed. And angry hens hissed, sticking out their strange worm-like tongues.

Dru leapt from bed. The bedroom door was closed on the chaos of her studio, which she had still not tidied, having no immediate new project.

She had no idea of trying to barricade the door. The door, and the inner walls of the bedroom, were only plasterboard, there for privacy, not protection. In any case she was driven now, pushed and pulled to look out, and to see.

The door, shoved, swung wide. Dru understood precisely what she was looking for. And there it was. Not, inevitably, where it had been, up on the sheet-draped bench, against the backdrop of the other sheet. It had got down from there, using whatever energy or agility powered it. Now it poised – or posed – at the room's centre. And through the windows the raw amber eyes of the municipal streetlights lit it without artistry, but in exact detail. The clock. The clock she and Jack and Pete had constructed for the photo-shoot, from odds and ends, bits and pieces. It did not now look like that at all. It looked – as she had made it look with Photoshop. The apparatus was three-dimensional and dense, consolidated and all-at-one.

In height, she estimated, it rose to nine feet, far bigger than the model. In appearance it was formed from gleaming basalt, and trimmed with bright metals and burnished wood representing suns and moons, vegetable briaries, flowers more like lilies than any Tudor Rose. Above it poked a sort of spike rather like the miniature spire of some cathedral, a gold, architectural lacework. There was only one omission – the one Dru herself had coined for its portrait. The clock had no face, no longer told time. And there inside the circular void something obscure was slowly blondly shifting and redly churning. Yet, unlike Dru's illustration, there was no hint in it of a human figure, neither girl nor stone. Rather, it was like a benighted and dissolving Martian world.

Last, last of all, her eyes ran downward to the base of the clock.

She had created this, and them. At least, their blue-print, these two creatures upon whose arched and sturdy spines the clock rested so intransigently. But they had far exceeded her imagination anyway. They had become themselves. Identical perhaps they were, and formed too partly of black stone and gold and silver, but also they were made of other colors, and of skin and horn, chitin, feathers. And scales. Such a lot of scales.

They were cockerels certainly, but their mere bodies alone some three feet in length. Their long necks, sinuous and serpentine, craned up into the prows of beaks like a kind of tortoiseshell striated golden, and on their heads the cock-crests were erect, (like the crests of dragons) not black or gold, but a dully shining henna red. Their eyes were like faceted glass. They glittered. They were full of sight. How many mathematical times inside those insect eyes was Dru replicated? The wings spread wide, held wide, black as the wings of ravens and crows. And below, the thick and corded, pine-bark branches of their blood-red legs, spurred with adamant, and the claws extended, hooks of steel.

As Dru stared at them, and at the towering clock, swaying and lumbering on their backs, (like that other earth, balanced on a turtle or toad) simultaneously they moved. For now they had her full attention. Cockatrices, Cocatrises, Cucutrixes, they gaped their beaks. She saw, in each of their mouths, two bladed lines of pointed teeth, black as obsidian and scintillant. And from the red caves of their gullets, the black worm-snakes of tongues quested, flickering. Out came the hiss. A double hiss. And she smelled the stench of them. Which was not like poultry, or tinder or guns – but like a putrefying wound. And at this signal, they each uncoiled their silver lizard-viper tails and lashed them, cat-like and furious, and mindless, pitiless.

She could not speak, let alone scream. She could not move hand or foot. She saw then they, the clock, composite of some Hell she had never believed existed, come running right at her, lurching and facile – eager.

Dru was aware she was about to be dead. She had forgotten her name. Death was almost on her, the lover, the wild beast, the Devil –

And the thing, clock and cockatrice, sprang past her, not upon, and flew up in the air in a sort of ignition, a spray of sparks, and a loud seismic rumbling. Straight through the biggest studio window it – they – went. The window shattering, a thousand fiery stars, a million cascading mirrors, less breakage than explosion. And over the tops of the streetlights Dru saw the horror sail, flapping and yawing like a storm-wracked galleon, up into the ceiling of the black motionless London sky, moonless and welcoming. For several more minutes she watched how they grew small and vanished, only with perspective, only into distance, and through the final loss of the orange light.

Jack was the one who shouted, Pete looked hurt. They had thought she might let them show the Cockatrice clock as part of a gallery exhibition they were putting together. They would have given her a proper credit, she knew that, made a reference to her piece in the magazine. "I suppose you had some mad drunk piss-up here and someone smashed it," snarled Jack.

She had not, of course, told them the truth. Or about the dream, if it was a dream. The nightmare. It was neither.

"I'm sorry, Jack. No one smashed it. There was no party. I was on my own here. I heard a crash and when I came out –"

"Then why was half of it in the fucking room and half down

on the fucking pavement?" howled Jack.

"Leave it, Jacky," said Pete, now looking worried. "Are you OK, Dru? You seem a bit shaky."

"No, I'm all right, thanks."

"But you nearly went over just then. Sit down. Jack doesn't mean –"

"Don't tell her what I mean!"

"Look, Jacky, look – she's shaken up. Can we get you some water, Dru? Cup of tea?"

But Jack only left, and Pete, murmuring soothing words, went with him. She was relieved, though she concluded they would never want to work with her again.

But what could she have said? It disintegrated the window and flew off over the roofs into outer space? The window, after all, was not broken, but quite intact. Only debris of so many sorts had been left lying all over the studio floor and, as Jack pointed out, down on the pavement below. That had been the worst to clear up. She had been threatened by the landlord with eviction. "Council won't stand for that, you know. Dodgy mess like that all over the street. D'you want to get me sued?"

Nothing of the clock had remained intact. It was entirely splinters and grains, like a peculiar muesli. And...feathers. But maybe they came from passing brunette pigeons. The clock was destroyed. Only its – what? Soul? Spirit? – had flown away. (She had wondered bemusedly if any of the endless security cameras had caught it. But even if they had, no one would believe a thing like that.) "It could do what it bloody well wanted," as Robert Trenchall said. And had done so.

Less than a week after, she read about him in a newspaper. Dru did not bother with papers as a rule, but this one was lying open on a wine-bar counter, as if put there for her.

They talked a lot about his music, his talent. A "loss" they called it, so young. He was only thirty-two.

Robert Trenchall had had, it seemed, a very public argument with his live-in lover, Susina Cruz, during which she had accused him of multiple infidelity and thrown the contents of a glass of champagne in his face. Guest tourists at the house, (Sessonby, the home of the late artist Vera Sylvia Reive) had not been unduly perturbed. Indeed, some confessed to amusement, and Trenchall himself, after some initial displeasure, had apparently laughed it off. But Ms. Cruz fled in a taxi to the airport and on to California. And next morning Trenchall was dead. There were no sinister implications either of murder or suicide. Though odd in an active and fit man of Trenchall's age, he had suffered a major stroke. The lifestyles of music and theatre were blamed, and drugs were hinted at, though nothing worse was noted in his system than wine. A single curious fact the papers failed to learn, and so did not report, was that his entire body, when first discovered, was completely rigid, not from rigor mortis, but as if, one of the medics remarked, filled with hardened cement. Or stone.

And it was three years more before Dru's then current lover exclaimed, there in the hotel room in Montmartre, "God, Dru! When did that happen?"

"What? Oh, this."

"Yes. That."

"I always forget about it."

"How can you forget?"

"Oh, it isn't like the big toe, you know. That can affect your balance seriously. But this. Well, you get used to not having it fairly fast."

"But what happened?"

"Accident. Something fell on it."

"What fell on it?"

"A clock."

At which the lover became nicely protective, and drew her into an embrace, the nature of which soon altered course.

By then Dru really was unfazed by the loss of the little toe on her left foot. It truly did not inconvenience her. But even after a few days without it, she had become used to its absence, only now and then making a misstep. And in a month or so that too was gone. The injury never caused her any pain either. She had never needed to seek medical attention. As well. Just as with Jack and Pete, what on earth could she have said? She had been amazingly fortunate, let off one could assume, very lightly. At the time, caught in the glare of the demon, she had believed all of her would petrify, like Diana Sesby. And maybe just like Robert Southurst's heart. But the cockatrice clock had spared her this. And that night, staggering back to bed, dropping down, passing out or only sleeping, she had not even guessed – let alone felt – the token payment that had been collected. She had known nothing at all until she got up the following morning, and took that first uneven, weirdly disgusting step. And looking down, saw. Or rather, did not see. There was no blood. No wound. Only the subtraction. She made it to the bathroom and threw up. Then she sat on the floor and studied her new foot, until she had grown used to it. At last, returning to the bed, Dru pulled off the covers, and searched until she found what, during oblivion, had simply snapped away.

It said something about her, she was sure, though God knew quite what, that she kept it afterwards, still did, in a small tin box that had originally held lemon-flavoured pastilles. Her toe, that was, perfect even to the tiny, once-painted toe-nail. And made thereafter, and now, not of perishable flesh and bone, but of the smoothest, coldest, greyest, and most impervious granite.

Malicious Springs

A chance phrase that came from nowhere: 'Hope springs eternal, but malice springs eternally' set before me the derivative title Malicious Springs. So how were they malicious? What form did the malice take? The environ and all the characters at once arrived, as they usually do. I confess too I always like the excellent Bill, and the wonderful Jacob.

They were rowed across the lake. It was milky blue-green-grey silk, and nothing on it but tiny islands green-meshed in trees, and far over there, a line of ducks cutting a white wake.

"There's something in the water," said Mr Perkins, the guy who was rowing the boat.

Everyone but Jacob stared over the side at the lake. "Where?" asked Elaina. Then, "What?" Mr Perkins said, "No, not that"

Bill was still interested. He said to Jacob, "*Hey.*" But Jacob only wagged his tail. Elaina laughed. And Dad said, "You mean like the Loch Ness Monster, Mr Perkins?" In that cool, ironic tone that annoyed so many people.

Mr Perkins though was impervious. He said, "I'm only repeating what I heard. The last lot stayed at the house, they said there was something in the water and it ought to be reported. They left early. Maybe they did report it But no one took no notice."

"Well, have *you* seen anything, Mr Perkins?" Your house is only across over there, isn't it, by the farm? Surely you might have? When you were fishing, perhaps."

"Don't go fishing," said Mr Perkins. "Don't hold with it." Silence returned. Mr Perkins had driven them up from the station, then through the village, allowing them a halt at the village shop for provisions, finally loaded their bags into the boat, and helped them in too. Elaina could have managed without any help, Shaw (Dad) was a bit clumsy. Bill and Jacob scrambled in, in a tangle of arms, legs and paws. Mr Perkins was that strange combination of taciturn and chatty. Half an hour would pass, then came some burst of information. "That's the church, see. Twelfth Century that is. There's the road to the shore. Lovely views." And now this about *something* in the water.

Bill peered down through the milky surface of the lake. His ten-year-old eyes were clear enough, the lake less so. He couldn't make out anything much – only some weed, floating. Not even fish.

But in a way it was a relief to have something else to think about. On the train, next in the car, all pressed together, he and Jacob and Elaina in the back, and Dad, the slightly well-known writer, sitting by Mr Perkins. Awkward.

It wasn't that Bill didn't like Elaina. She was friendly, pretty and quite young, at least nine years younger than Dad, and Dad had been much happier, less cold and preoccupied, since she had become part of his life. But Elaina was – awkward. She was so determined not to try to *take his mother's place* with Bill, that it made both Bill and herself uneasy. The holiday here, at this rented house by the lake, was for Dad to settle down and finish the latest novel. And for them all to 'spend time together'. Bill assumed too this was a dress rehearsal for Shaw and Elaina – and Bill – living together permanently. Or at least until something else happened, as it had three years ago, when Mum had dumped both Shaw and Bill, and left, as Shaw put it, "On a fucking jet-plane."

"There's the house up there, see," announced Mr Perkins.

"The white one? Oh yes," cried Elaina, "I recognise it from the brochure."

"Nice house that. Eighteenth century."

"And it has, let's see, an acre of apple orchard, its own well, and an oak staircase with carved banister," finished Elaina. Shaw smiled. "What do you think, Bill?"

"Looks good," said Bill, encouragingly. It seemed all right, the house, perched up there over the trees. He wondered if it would be possible to spot the Lake Ness Monster from those bay windows at the front. It looked a steepish climb to get there, and Dad would get out of breath and try to pretend he hadn't.

When the boat grounded on the pebbles below the steps, Jacob shot off like a black and brown rocket.

"Jake! Come back!" yelled Shaw, waving his arms in panic. "Bloody dog– he'll have himself lost."

But Jacob only ran up into the trees, barked a bit, then ran back grinning, to see why the rest of his pack was taking so long to join him.

By early evening, they had, Shaw said, claimed their terrain. Elaina, who seemed to like domestic stuff, had made up the beds, and generally reorganised the house, moving couches, scattering extra cushions, arranging candles, putting flowers into vases. Now she was constructing hamburgers from local meat, while Shaw dealt with the salad and cooled two bottles of white wine in the fridge.

Bill did like the house. It had two storeys, with four large rooms and kitchen and scullery on the ground floor, and two winding corridors upstairs, in some parts going up an extra two or three steps, that rambled through another set of rooms.

The views of the lake were wonderful. Even Bill, the pragmatist, could see they were, but best of all, the windows seemed perfect for monster spotting. Dad's chosen 'study' above, however, looked inland to the orchard. "I have to keep my eyes on the computer keys, Bill. The lake's too interesting. But you and Elaina must go for lots of walks." At which Elaina and Bill glanced uncomfortably at each other, and then beamed, to show how great that would be.

Dad was selfish. Bill knew that because Shaw had often said so. 'I'm a writer. It makes you selfish.'

Jacob loved the orchard He and Bill had run about there for an hour, then come in thirsty. Elaina, efficiently, already had Jacob's water-bowl down and filled, and a large orange juice in the fridge for Bill.

Shaw washed lettuce and tomatoes at the stone sink. Bill opened a jar of green olives and hooked out two. He noticed Jacob staring at him. Jacob had that funny look in his eyes he got sometimes. Then he sneezed and ran out of the open scullery door, across the little yard there, and back into the orchard.

"That dog is possessed," said Shaw. He sometimes took pride in Jacob's eccentricities.

"You're wrong," said Elaina, "he just likes to be in a big garden for a change."

Bill could see Jacob. He hadn't gone far. He seemed to be jumping about in a rather odd way. Then he came bounding back, grinning, rushed into the kitchen and leapt straight up on the surface where Elaina was working at the hamburgers.

Everyone yelled. Elaina shrieked with outraged surprise as Jacob wolfishly ripped a chunk of the compressed meat from her hand. Then, like a whirlwind, Jacob fled back out of the door.

"Are you all right? He didn't bite you, did he?"

"No – no – it just –"

"He doesn't do that sort of thing."

Bill wanted to laugh, but didn't. Elaina still looked slightly upset, as if maybe this had happened because she had offended Jacob. She took things too personally. If he had been able, Bill would gently have explained that to her.

"Well, that dog gets no supper tonight," proclaimed Shaw. "I said, he's possessed. He acts half the time as if he has a through-line to some sort of deranged dog-god."

Now Elaina laughed, and relaxed. "It's OK. There's lots left. What he stole will do him more good than canned dog food."

"Don't make excuses for the brute."

Jacob, disgraced, didn't return. The humans sat to eat in the last summery light, out on the honey-suckled veranda at the front of the house. Golden sparkles crystalled the lake, and long shadows spread purple there from the tree-hung islets. Nothing rose save a single duck, wheeling away into the westering sun.

"It's beautiful here," said Elaina.

They agreed the food was good. The hot meat and crusty bread from the local shop were first class. The salad too, though Bill had managed to avoid eating most of that. The French wine also seemed to do Elaina and Shaw good as it usually did. Bill drank his orange juice, wondering with fond contempt what it was adults liked so much about booze. Pretty awful he thought it, the couple of times they had let him try.

"More salad, Bill? Thought not. I'll get coffee. Then I think showers and bed."

Unimpressed by talk of showers, Bill considered the idea of coffee. He didn't get that either very often, but at least it was a drink worth having.

In the night, Bill woke up and heard them arguing. This hadn't happened before, not with Elaina, though she had once or twice stayed at the house in London. With Mum it had happened more or less non-stop, ending in the time she flung a kettle of just-off boiling water at Dad. He had dodged most of it, but by the time Shaw and Bill got back from the hospital, Mum was gone for good.

So Bill didn't like the sound of a row. He lay rigid in the holiday bed, between the clean sheets, with a white moon shining in at the thin curtains, and no Jacob to grab hold of.

"I tell you you're too young to understand, you silly little bitch."

"Shaw – if I'm so fucking *young,* what am I doing with *you?*"

Oh Christ, thought Bill. Please stop it. Please God, make them stop.

Perhaps God, busy though He must be, had a moment, because now the voices went lower, kinder. "Shit, Elly. Sorry. I don't know. I'm just tired – and that book – you know the trouble I'm having with Chapter Seven."

"OK. It's all right. Sweety, you know I love you?"

Then murmurs too low to decipher. Presently the carefully quiet-because-Bill-may-hear sounds of loving sex. Bill didn't ever mind those, even though they were as alien to him as Mars. They were happy, even funny, sounds. It was just arguments he didn't like. They – scared him. "Thanks, God." Bill was a polite boy.

About two hours later, when dawn was starting to drift from the land towards the lake, another noise – much louder and weirder – woke everyone.

Bill sat upright, and when he heard his father charging down the stairs with Elaina behind him, Bill sprang up and also ran in the same direction.

Back in London, Jacob never stayed out at night. He slept with Bill, usually. Here, as the dog hadn't returned, despite Elaina's cooing from the scullery yard, they had left him to it. Even Bill did that, since he trusted Jacob to be invincible. And now, Jacob *was* back. He had got in, they reasoned, at a window left ajar in the front room.

After which he reached the kitchen, and was currently throwing himself at the fridge door. On the stone floor nearby, his water-bowl lay broken in pieces, water pooling dark as blood.

"Jesus – Shaw – you don't think he's rabid, do you?"

"I hope not. We're not supposed to have it over here – Jacob – calm *down* – what the hell's the matter?"

Jacob stopped bouncing at the fridge door. He turned insane glowing eyes upon them and let out a crackling yowl.

"Maybe he's hurt-"

"Don't go to him, El, let me do it."

Bill said in a high desperate voice, "Dad, open the fridge."

"Don't be crazy. He's not some desperate kid with hunger pangs he's a dog –"

"Hang on," said Elaina. "Let's just see." She sidled by Jacob, who let her, abruptly looking more worried than dangerous, wagging his tail as she pulled open the door. Then she threw herself back as Jacob leapt once more, straight up against the packed compartment.

"He's after the bloody hamburgers again –"

Jacobs's long paws and long nose flailed in amongst ketchup

and salads. The half-filled second wine bottle, left from dinner, teetered at the onslaught. It tilted slowly, pondering whether to fall out or not. Then fell. It smashed on the floor, and wine spread in another puddle.

Jacob slid from the fridge, lowered his head and lapped up the wine.

"Jake, stop that – it's full of broken glass – what's the matter with the stupid fool?" Shaw now had Jacob by the collar, hauling him away. Jacob, docile, tail-wagging, permitted this. Shaw sat on a kitchen chair, holding Jacob's head between his hands, staring in Jacob's liquid eyes. "My God, we have an alcoholic dog."

"I'm off for a walk around the lake. May visit the farm shop. Want to come?"

Bill glanced dubiously at Elaina, all bright, trying to be a good friend but *not* in his mother's place. Hovering at the breakfast table, Shaw was looking miserable, wanting, or afraid, to get back to his difficult Chapter Seven. There had been another row. A quick flash-flood of one. About the bloody muesli. And Bill had sat there, his mouth dry as bone. Only Jacob, cool and reasonable once more and leaning on Bill's leg, helped him keep together. Now he would have to act like he wanted to go with Elaina. "Sure," he said, smiling radiantly. "Can Jacob come?"

"He'd better," said Elaina, "needs some fresh air for that hangover."

Outside, as they started off along the brow of the hill, Jacob – not at all hungover – bounding through the trees, tall grass and wild flowers, Elaina paused. "Bill, you know it's OK with Shaw and me? I know it's rotten to hear us shout like that – don't know why we did – but we don't mean it, Bill. We – *like* each other, your Dad and me. Okay?"

"OK," said Bill. She was a nice woman, trying to reassure him. But he had seen their eyes – like Jacob's, actually, when he thieved the hamburgers, or when he knocked the bottle out of the fridge. Going upstairs to clean his teeth, Bill had passed

Shaw's study. Shaw stood by his computer, drinking from a half bottle of whisky. Seeing Bill see, Shaw shrugged guiltily. "Swift nip, sir, prior to embarkation on writer's block." Bill had nodded and gone on to the bathroom. He hadn't seen Shaw drink like that in the morning since the Mum days.

Though Bill conscientiously cleaned his teeth, he hadn't showered. Last night he hadn't taken a bath either, though one had been run for him. In London he was fairly strict with himself, but here – well, it was a holiday. He didn't stink yet. He used the bottle of Evian to rinse his mouth of toothpaste, as they did at home. He had meant to get a cup of coffee off Shaw this morning, but the row had prevented that. So it had just been juice. If this farm shop was any good, he might persuade Elaina to buy him a Pepsi.

The walk was fine, at first. Oak trees splashed up green into the blue sky. The red flowers in the grass were poppies, apparently, and the pink-white ones ox-eye daisies.

Jacob too seemed fine now. It was all fine. Then, without warning, Elaina started to cry.

This was worse because at first she had tried to hide it, then pretend she wasn't, then she said, "Sorry, Bill. Shit, really sorry. I'm all right. Sorry, Bill."

Bill remembered his mother, crying. Drunk and crying. Slapping Dad And Dad shouting, and then crying too. Dad drinking whisky. And then the boiled water flying through the air, and Dad shaking with shock, trying to drive safely to A and E. And saying to a nurse, "Dropped the bloody kettle. Stupid."

Jacob found a rabbit. Jacob chased the rabbit.

"For fuck's sake – leave it alone – that fucking dog – I'll *kill* it –"

'That's Jacob –"

"I know who it fucking – look – do you want to see a rabbit chomped right there in the grass in front of you? *I* don't." "He won't. He won't catch up." "How do you know? What rabbits are there in London?"

"There *are*. On the heath."

"Christ's sake shut up, Bill."

Jacob lost the rabbit. Elaina left off shouting. Bill felt sick. They went on around the lake. After about twenty minutes, she said, "God, Bill. Sorry." "S'okay."

"I don't know what – it must be PMT."

Bill knew what PMT was, though he didn't *understand* what it was. His mother had always been blaming it for her moods. But Elaina didn't have moods – Elaina was always too worried about upsetting someone –

"Look, there's the farm. And there's Mr perky Perkins's house, that red one up by the wooded bit. Hey, maybe the farm sells ice-cream."

The farm shop was by the gate of the farm. Beyond, flowed sloping summer fields, with cream rolled up rugs on legs – sheep. The other way, the hill curved down to a craggy path, and so to the strand of the lake. The shop was open, and sold everything on Earth.

Jacob took no notice.

The moment they reached the brink of the downward path, the dog scooted away. Bill was terrified Elaina would lose her temper again, and when she didn't, and simply looked concerned, Bill suggested he should follow the dog down. It was a relief to get away. "Ice-cream ready when you come back!" she cried after him.

Bill trekked down the path, through the cascades of oak and beech. He couldn't see the beauty, not even the potential, now. It was just a green place, full of trouble. He found Jacob at the water's edge, drinking and drinking as if about to consume the lake.

"She put you out a new bowl. It was the big cereal one. Didn't you remember to drink the water?"

It was like taking a pee before you left the house. Or washing your hands– which Bill thought he hadn't done, had he?

But yes, he had, only using the hygienic moistened tissues. He liked those. They smelled like doctor's stuff. He had liked doctors ever since the kettle and A and E. They had been kind, to Dad, and to Bill.

When Jacob at last stopped drinking, they trolled back up the slope. Birds sang and called in the woods. Just noises. There had been nothing eventful to see in the water.

Elaina had another bag full of items for meals. She handed Bill a can of Pepsi *and* a chocolate ice-cream. He stood holding them, now disabled – both hands lost to him – not wanting either treat anymore. But he would have to eat and drink them. Not only not to make her feel bad – not to get her *angry*. Yes, he remembered the safety drill for that.

Jacob though, helped out. When Bill managed to drop it, the dog wolfed the ice-cream. Elaina saw, and a moment of fear resulted, but she only laughed after all. "Do you want another one, Bill? Go on, you can. It wasn't your fault."

Not much. "No thank you."

Elaina was drinking cola too. The fat woman in the white blouse leaned over the counter, smiling at them all.

"Yes, they left in a great hurry. Sometimes happens, see. People – they get out of their depth."

"Mr Perkins – he rowed us across – he said they said there was something in the lake?"

"In the lake? I never. Well, I don't know what that could be. Nothing there but a few ducks and fishes. The water, see," said the white-bloused woman, "that comes in from the river, and goes on to the sea. Bit of a coming back, there. The lake, it's just a bit salty, mind. You *can* drink it. But the best water's up on the hills. Sweet as sugar. Every house has its own well. There's the Holly Well and the Black Ram Well and the Century Well over by the shore road. Water clean as anything, it is. Better than the tapped muck in the town."

Elaina leaned in too, towards the counter. "What well is ours, at the white house?"

"Oh, that well isn't much, I'm afraid. Dried out that well is. Your water comes up from the town, pipes to the taps. Sorry to disappoint."

"Yeah," said Elaina. "And I thought it had a bit of a kick to it, our water. Kidding myself."

"A kick? There's a funny thing now."

Walking back was better. Elaina began to talk to Bill about Shaw, just gently, confiding. Bill liked it, to hear his father so comprehended, forgiven and adored Was it safe now, then?

"I've been very good," said Shaw, at lunch. "I've done five hundred words." He still looked gloomy. When things were going right, he could skate through two and a half thousand words in a morning. "One interesting line I came up with – listen –" he picked up his longhand notebook, and read: "Maybe hope springs eternal, but malice springs eternally.' What do you think, Elly?"

"Ironic and nasty. Strong."

"I thought so too. Have to place it right, the line, but it's very pertinent to the text. But, well, I did read a bit, too. About the rivers here. There's a guidebook in the bookshelf.

Lunch was sandwiches, thick chunks of ham and sliced tomatoes. Bill managed to wiggle the tomatoes out and lose them. He took an apple though, and carried it off to eat, then left it somewhere, uneaten.

After lunch, Shaw and Elaina departed upstairs for a rest. Bill thought it was really for sex. That was fine.

He went into the kitchen and looked at Jacob, nosing at his water-bowl, not drinking it. Jacob grunted, shovelling the bowl about.

Bill went to the fridge, got out the Evian, tipped the tap-water down the sink, and filled the bowl again from the bottle. Once he set it down Jacob lowered his head and lapped.

Standing watching, Bill cautiously sniffed at himself. Nothing, he thought, but... he might be wrong. He took another bottle of Evian from the fridge and carried it to the bathroom, where he twice filled the basin, and washed himself all over, thoroughly. He had heard of actors who refused to wash their hair or bathe in ordinary water. Was that why he had done it?

He turned on the tap and let the ordinary water run through, the water everyone else in the house was using for tea and coffee, cleaning fruit and vegetables, and for having baths and showers.

From the bedroom came soft seethings. Poor Martians. He had to take care of them.

Bill craned forward and stared up at the gushing tap. He was about to reach up and stick his tongue under the flow, when Jacob padded into the room. The growl that burst from the dog could have come from prehistory. It was dark and horrible, lawless, menacing and full of fear. Bill stood up. He put his hand, one finger, towards the running water. Jacob snarled, his lip peeled back from healthy gums and ice-white shark's teeth. "What is it?" Bill asked softly. But Jacob had never learned to talk. When Bill turned off the tap, Jacob came and leaned against him, raising his eloquent head to be caressed.

Along the hall in the bedroom, Elaina gave a thin, wavering scream. It was only sex, but normally she kept so quiet, for Bill's sake. Maybe they thought he was out in the orchard.

He kissed Jacob between the eyes and they went down, silently as clever burglars, through the house, and out by the scullery door.

The old well was in the orchard, covered by a movable lid, slung round with ivy. Bill climbed up the step and pushed the lid. He peered over into a rusty nothing, and Jacob, running up next to him, paws on the rim, peered in too. Jacob seemed interested, but not upset.

The well was dry.

From the house, through the open window, voices.

"Oh stop it, Elaina. Just be quiet. I'll work later, when it's cooler."

"I only said —"

"You're nagging. Why? Concerned I can't earn any more

44

money, that it? Stuck with an old man who can't keep you in Chardonnay and fucking Alpen."

"Christ. What is it with you? You are getting to be a pain, Shaw – *Shaw let go of me, you bastard –*"

Bill and Jacob sprinted along the orchard, through the extending shadows of the three o'clock trees. The embryos of apples hung above them. Through trunks they glimpsed hills, distant isolated houses, the flat shine of the lake.

He had only once been seriously late home. That time he had been avoiding a couple of kids, and got lost on the edge of the heath after school. Dad came along later, with torches and two neighbours, calling. Bill hadn't meant to frighten Shaw. Now, Bill didn't consider that. He shut them both, his father, the woman, from his mind. And with them, the sound of the slap he had heard ringing from the bedroom window.

Bill and Jacob ran through the orchard and the afternoon, and wandered across the hills, down to the lip of the lake. There they played desperately, as if very, very happy, in the deepening golden light. When the sun moved over beyond the hills, mauve shadows dipped the shore. The lake turned to pale smooth metal, lit by one long last warm sun-ray. Then everything sighed to a luminous dimness, and stars began to appear on the dark blue sky.

By now Bill was hungry. So, doubtless, was Jacob. Bill sat skimming pebbles out across the lake. He couldn't make them bounce. Jacob sat by his side, panting, not complaining.

Night unfolded its wings.

"How's it happen?" Bill asked Jacob. Jacob looked at him attentively, listening, considering. "Is it the well?" If Jacob knew – very likely he *did* – he couldn't say.

What time was it? The moon had come and was going over and Bill, who had left his watch behind in the bathroom, guessed the hour was almost 9pm.

Normally by now, dinner had been eaten, dishes seen to.

Maybe they would have had some TV, reading, or a game – chess, or *Galactic Grab* on Dad's computer. Bath and bed looming. Bill was tired. Tonight he wouldn't have been sorry to be sent to bed. Should they sleep down here? Bill stared about him. There were creeping shades along the shore, which might be anything. Though they had misunderstood what Mr Perkins had said – or indeed Mr Perkins himself misunderstood what he heard – there might anyway be – *things* – in the lake, which only surfaced by night. Could any of those be worse than what might be happening in the house on the hill? Torn between the proper and instructive terrors of youth, and the deadly horror-terror of real life, Bill started to cry. Jacob shoved in close. Bill held the dog, breathed courage in from his coat, and closed the sluice-gates of his eyes with a sharp pain against the tears. "We'd better go back, Jacob. See how it is, eh? Can't be so bad. Maybe it's OK now. Maybe it wasn't so bad – maybe."

Boy and dog walked back along the shore, and found the steps that rose up to the white house. No one had come to look for them. Or – had searchers gone in another direction?

They ran up the steps, up the hill.

This way, coming to the house from the front, it towered up suddenly, foreshortened, unnerving – *black*. For there weren't any lights on, not in the upper rooms nor the bay windows of the front facade. On the unlighted veranda, the table and chairs had an intense stasis. If anybody had ever had dinner tonight, the table had been monumentally cleared – last night, they hadn't been so tidy. On the other hand, they hadn't, last night, knocked over any chairs, and now one lay on its side. A rose, shattered from the vine, covered the ground below like flakes of white paper.

They had gone out. They must have done. Out looking for Bill. That was it.

New panic enfolded the old leaden panic of the afternoon.

On the top step, below the slope of the hill that led up to the veranda, Bill stood, gazing in darkness, on darkness. And that was when Jacob began, deep in his guts, to growl like a nightmare wolf.

From nowhere – sound and fury, movement and threat. The front door crashed open and light blazed out of the hallway, slicing the veranda down the middle, and the night, and Bill's eyes. And through the light, a roar of a voice, not really human, like some demon in a movie – Words, but not properly words, rage unable to decipher itself. It was Shaw. Bill could just make him out through the blinding light, just make out his voice through the demon roaring.

"Sorry –" Bill faltered. He wanted to turn and run, or run to his father and have his father change at once back into – a father.

But the combination demon-man came blundering out and reached for Bill. Then Bill *heard* the words, "Little fucking bastard – get inside –" and a foot kicking out, all the weight of the body behind it, at Jacob – who, instinct honed from the caves of his ancestral past, leapt from its way, and half lay, belly flat to the grass, snarling. For Bill, true reaction had already been too far subsumed by ordinary life. *He* was already caught. Hauled into the house. The door slammed Three centuries of stone and timber quaked – probably not for the first time.

They were in the front room, and again light slammed on and Elaina was lying there in a chair, her face bruised and her nails broken and her eyes mad, rising up, screaming at both of them.

On the low table were glasses and a glass jug. They had been drinking – what was it? – not wine, not lemon barley water. No. Clear, the glass. Shiny. Water. They had been drinking water. From the tap.

Shaw pushed his son aside. Bill stared up and saw this face that was a devil's and the tortured eyes he remembered, which howled for help from miles away.

Elaina spoke slurringly, as if very drunk.

"I'm thirsty. Go on, you parasitic little git, fill that jug None of the shit from the bottles. Get it out the fucking taps, d'ya hear?"

"Yes," said Bill. He seized the jug, and ran by his father who, in that extreme moment, seemed dementedly to try to strike Bill even as he passed. But the blow missed, the passage and the kitchen door were gained.

Darkness was still there.

Bill stood breathing. Perhaps they might forget they had sent him on this mission. But no. They would crave what he must bring them. He had only a moment Bill crossed to the sink, put in the plug, and turned the tap full on. As his night-vision once more adjusted, half turning, he saw the head of Jacob appear wolf-like against the starry kitchen window pane, and heard the dog's body slam against the frame.

Then and only then, there in the dark, refined by the worst fear on earth, terror of those you love, Bill saw it. Saw what was in the water.

A narrow sound scraped out of his throat. Was this a bad dream? Never. Bill was a child, even he grasped that he was, and children know, and children still *see* – as animals generally do, (unless too corrupted by proximity to mankind) and other creatures who retain their higher sight.

This then was why only he had, this altruistically obedient boy, instinctively avoided shower and bath, even washing his hands with wipes, rinsing his mouth with Evian, not eating any salad, dropping what they thought he *had* eaten off the veranda, unseen, not biting into an apple. Even the coffee he believed he had *wanted*, he hadn't got. Water. Everything had been washed in it. Fruit and veg, human skins – or it was in the kettle for the tea and coffee, mixed in the lemon and barley drink – going straight in at every orifice or little cut, and through the intestines by the mouth itself, that infallible door. Tiding like the sea.

They were like bubbles made of mercury, the things in the water, about the size, he thought, of pound coins. *Easily* big enough to see – once you could see them. If ever you did. And they were hard and firm, yet flexible, and they moved, gleaming, rubbing against each other, attaching and subdividing and making more and more, so the whole sheet of the sinkful of water, the gush from the tap, were like a fountain and a lake of miniature silver *worlds*. But they were like microbes too. Huge microbes. Like amoebas seen in the biology book. And they were the seeds of some ancient evil, come up from the elder spring under the hill, bypassing cunningly the dried well, entering instead, by some little chip or hairline fracture of the modern pipes, the hermetic public water sent from the town.

The two out there were bellowing. They didn't sound at all human, more like frightened cattle. Bill thought, a bull stung by wasps –

He filled the water jug from the tap, almost halfway. There was a new bottle of white wine in the fridge. It wasn't open. There was no time. At the window now Jacob was barking and howling, scratching, scrabbling, trying to claw down the wall–

Bill smashed off the top of the bottle of wine. He hoped no glass fell down in it, but only out on the floor. He slopped the wine into the water. And, in the dark, watched the things that were in the water writhing – bursting – disintegrating – dying. When they had completely vanished, he heard Jacob fall silent. The dog was grinning in at him, pleased that his lesson had been well-taught.

Bill ran into the front room. Two Neanderthal beings in jeans came rampaging at him. He dodged them and sloshed the dead water and curative wine into their glasses. Then they rushed for those. Would they notice a faint tawny tinge, an alcoholic bouquet? What would happen now, if they drank? Would they too die?

After a few minutes Bill sat down on the couch. He sat watching them. He watched them come back, Dad and Elaina. They returned dazed, and abruptly drunk, pissed out of their minds yet quiet, rational. They were bewildered. Yet they didn't forget the prelude. They gaped at it in retrospect, and at Bill, and stammered things. They wandered about the room. Shaw staggered over and stroked Bill's hair. Bill held himself like stone not to shiver. By eleven-thirty he felt able to get up and bring the rest of the wine bottle, then let Jacob back into the house. Jacob padded patiently into the front room too, and sat by Bill, as they watched

Though they tried often to speak to Bill, Bill would only nod. He was their judge. Mostly aware of what had occurred, they accepted this fact. They respectfully left Bill to judge them, he and the dog.

Near morning, they went, the man and woman, to the fridge. Brought in the case of Evian and some cans of Pepsi. When morning really came, everyone ate bread and butter and drank orange juice. They didn't talk at all. No one took a bath or shower.

Later each of them slept, there in the chairs, and Bill on the couch, Jacob next to him, head on Bill's knees.

Aeons after, voices drifted across Bill's sleep. She. He. These known strangers.

"Did we? Was it? I? You? What shall we do?"

"Forgive. Don't forget."

"But it must be reported. It's – poisonous – what *is* it?"

"Some hallucinogen – chemical filth. Or natural – unnatural. Maybe always here. Maybe in the old days – Twelfth Century, Eighteenth – they could handle it." "But we can't just – not –"

"No one believed anyone. The 'other lot' as Perkins put it, probably tried the police. And the police didn't believe them. Or they didn't bother. Or it was hushed up. And you know what they can be like, these sort of – hate to say it, but *parochial* people. Take our money, despise us. We're tourists. Enemies. No doubt they think our sort – we either survive, or we don't."

"But what we – what –"

"It can't happen again, away from here. We have to believe that And... make *him* believe it."

"Bill. Poor Bill. Oh God, Shaw."

"Don't cry. OK cry. I'll join you. But when he wakes up, we *stop.*"

In sleep, Bill was running with Jacob. Running up a mountain of years – ten – twelve – sixteen and away and away, (the woman and the man left far below for ever) and right over the top, Jacob and he, together and alone.

They were rowed across the lake the other way.

"Shame you got to go so soon. Business, was it?

"That's right, Mr Perkins."

"And a lovely day, and good weather forecast all month. And your missus's face all bruised where she fell down the oak stair – lucky nothing broken And lost your deposit on the stay, too. There's a pity."

Elaina looked grimly through her sunglasses at the receding hills. Shaw looked silently into his thoughts. Bill, with Jacob watching like a feral yet benign henchman, stared only down into the milky silk of the lake, blue-green-grey. Mr Perkins, for all his words of commiseration, seemed slightly to be smiling, maybe only at the sunlight, and the perfect tranquillity of the day.

The Greyve

This one resulted, only just before handing in the collection, from the actual title: Cold Grey Stones. I found the idea of the visitation irresistible, and wrote the story in about three hours. The name was simply there as well, no choice. The ending took me aback.

A headstone has appeared in my room.

It is of a pale slaty shade, and smooth, perhaps marble. There is a certain wet slickness to its surface. Engraved, it carries only two words, a name: Edward Grey. Not mine.

Just as a fire would warm the area, so the headstone makes the room very cold – more like an open refrigerator, probably.

This is a horrible room, anyway – all I can afford after I lost, sequentially, my job, my home, my wife. The ceiling sags and sometimes bits of it sprinkle the worn disgusting carpet like sugar. The bed is both too hard and too soft, in separate pockets. I get backache already and I've only been here six months. And I'm only forty-two for God's sake. The walls are – what is it – whitewashed, I suppose. Down the hall the shared bathroom is somewhere generally to avoid. After all, serving seven to ten people as it does, it's a public toilet, and like several of those, occasionally full of unsavoury things, such as spent needles. Enough of this description.

The headstone, incidentally, does not carry the name of any of my enemies – my useless brother, or the man who told me I was redundant. Not even the bloody PM, or the damnable chancellor. Not even my erstwhile so-called bank manager. I don't know the name. I've puzzled over it. No answer.

Am I freaked out by the headstone?

Well, I should be, probably. But there's been so much rubbish. So much Kafka-esque surreality. I think maybe I merely have weirdness-fatigue.

So I only accept the stone in the corner. I even greet it, when I come in from a walk round the park, or my visit to the benefits office. When I say greet, perhaps I mean *salute*. The way you're meant to with magpies, to avoid disaster.

And it sits there, and then I switch on the tiny TV, and it and I watch the news.

The landlord dropped in today. This doesn't often happen, but anyhow I think he does it less to catch us out in something – let alone help with anything – than to gloat.

Glancing about, he saw the headstone.

"Oh, that back then?" he asked. I said nothing. He said, "Thought the previous bloke took it with him. Must've," he informed himself, "hidden it, but then you finds it and lugs it out again."

"It just appeared," I told him.

"That's what he says," the landlord said. "Reckon one of them other buggers're playing about. Number 3 or 6. Get your lock changed, I would," he said, benignly. "Just make sure you drop a set of the new keys in for me at the shop –" he also owns the chippy on the corner – "that'll do."

Again I didn't reply. I couldn't afford to be extravagant with a locksmith, a new lock and two sets of keys. Besides, I have nothing left worth stealing. The government etc: stole all that last year.

It has moved.

The headstone of Edward Grey has come out into the room and is now standing at the foot of the lumpy bed, as if peering over the raggedy quilt at me or my absence.

I confronted it on waking this morning. It must have crept silently across in the night.

Rather than jump out of my skin, as in the best horror movie I should have done, I just lay there looking at it, as – apparently – it stood looking back at me.

"What do you want?" I inquired.

The headstone said nothing. Aside obviously from its permanent message of *Edward Grey*.

Presumably it's a haunt, indigenous to my room, unless it ever crops up elsewhere in the house. Would I have heard of it if it had? Some of them are so far gone, too, no doubt they would take it for just one more 'trip' – if that's still the current jargon.

I coined a new name for the headstone as I washed and shaved at the little sink of my Lilliputian kitchenette. Mr Grey made a nice neat pun with the headstone's true purpose. It belonged on a grave. So, it became the *Greyve*.

I told the headstone its new name.

If it was going to stay with me, after all I might as well have something individual to call it by. While I was out, I wondered if it would take the opportunity to move again. Maybe it always did, when I wasn't there, gliding silently round the room, staring at shelves and at the cracks in the walls, or even out of the window.

When I returned that evening, I looked up at my window, but the stone wasn't gazing out. When I let myself into the room though, it had indeed changed position. It was right by the cupboard so I couldn't get to my dinner can of baked beans. I considered what I would do if it next parked itself right by the door. The door opens into the room, so I wouldn't be able to get out past the Greyve. But there would be an exit possible via the window, after all, the drop only about ten feet. Two years ago that would have been nothing to me. I could probably still manage it, if I had to.

While I made my beanless cheese on toast and drank my single special-offer-reduced weak beer, I told the Greyve about these hypothetical methods, its move and my response.

And today, when I woke, it was standing firmly in front of the door.

My back certainly didn't seem to like the acrobatics into the front garden, but otherwise I was fine. I took my keys out with me, despite the fact I would not be able to get in again if the Greyve stayed where it then was. The window I'd managed to close as I wobbled on the windowsill –

thank God for a wide sill and a sash frame.

My reason for coming out: I meant to look up a former fellow-worker of mine, Bill Joins. Though made redundant three weeks after I was, Bill had made better Plans B, was not married, and had a connection or two. He had, back then, tried to get me work as well, but that fell through – I wasn't what the new firm wanted. Then he had slipped me a couple of grand – literally slipped – pick-pocketing it into my coat. After which I found it, called him, thanked him, said I couldn't take it, was persuaded to take it, (just a 'loan') and so on. After that, unable to repay him as skint, and afraid my turning up again in his life would make him think I was on a second handout mission, I hadn't gone near him.

This, however, was different.

I'd smartened myself up a bit, and taken out some cash I couldn't afford to, so as to buy my round.

Bill could generally be found at lunch time at the Pig and Hamper off Kensit Walk, eating a baguette and drinking one stiff glass of Merlot. I took the bus there, and went in, and there he was, as if only a week, not nearly two years, had flowed between us and away.

"Hi, Bill."

"Well hi – how are you doing – ?"

"Not so bad," I lied jauntily, "things are starting to look up. It's slow, but I'm hopeful." I tried to make it sound just good enough he wouldn't feel a need to hide his wallet, but not so good he'd get the wallet out and ask if I could repay his 'loan'.

But Bill's clever. He gave me just one thoughtful look. Then, tactful too, he started off on another lighter subject -the tennis, I think. We got our lunch. Finally, after I'd bought my round – Bill agreed to a spritzer – he reprised, "But you're doing OK?"

I grabbed my cue. "All but one thing. The place I'm living in is haunted."

"How intriguing. And that's a flat, is it, or –"

"Just a room. But it's ideal for where I need to be for the moment. Only difficulty is the haunt."

"Male or female?"

"Neither. Well, male maybe, but not in the usual sense."

"Really?"

I told Bill what it was.

He let out a laugh of pure amazement, or disbelief. Then, seeing my solemn face, he quietly said, "OK. So fill me in

I got back quite late. I'd gone for a walk through the old familiar London streets of my previous working and solvent life, which induced a kind of soft black mood, more sad than harsh.

The sun had gone and the late summer dusk was coming on when I eventually reached my present... home.

Aside from mulling over what Bill had said to me, I'd been thinking that I'd be a fool to sleep on that back-trap bed tonight. My ungainly plunge from window to garden had resulted in two or three knife-sharp twinges of pain, after which my spine had felt completely OK for the first time in months. It would be a shame to ruin this inadvertent and entirely free chiropracty. I'd do better to sleep on the floor –

In fact the conundrum had already been decided for me. I didn't know until I got in.

I had gone up to the door in the usual way, hoping the Greyve had grown bored and shifted position again. It had. As the key turned and I pushed, the door opened with its normal crunchy swing.

Blurred and dull with twilight, the room was obscure. I could see only dark shapes of things that mere pragmatic familiarity told me were the bed, the table and two chairs, the cupboard, the kitchinette units. Even so, I realized instantly I couldn't make out the Greyve.

Swiftly I hit the light switch.

Definitely I did *not* want any more surprises. However, I received one.

For sure, the Greyve was not *standing* anywhere in the room. Instead it was lying down. It was lying down on my bed, its stony head on my pillow.

Bill had told me he reckoned the name on the headstone, whatever the hell the headstone *itself* was, was some kind of code. So we'd had coffee and tried a few possibles. It seemed he didn't need to get back to work at all that afternoon, and his live-in girlfriend would be at her mother's until 5 o'clock. We came up with some odd anagrams. For example *Re: Dreg Ward* (from some phantom hospital no longer – or not *yet* – on the site." A non-anagram for this was also added: *E.D.* – standing for Emergency Decontamination – *Ward, Grey* (wing). Or there was the startled US *Gee! Dry Ward!* and the Olde Worlde disgusted *Gad, dry ewer!* We postulated too the literary conjure *Day grew red,* and a dispirited *Dry ragweed.* These were amusing, at the time. Alcohol *and* good coffee, plus a decent sandwich, had gone to my head.

He suggested I try my computer, let it work out all the possible letter/word permutations. And I had to 'explain' that, so far, I only used the one at 'work', and had better not fool around on it. I still hadn't replaced my machine at home, you see, etc: Bill obligingly said he'd try the anagram-code on his. And if I didn't object, he could ask a few friends their thoughts – he'd pass it off as a peculiar word puzzle, some game.

His main premise was, however, that the headstone, though no doubt I *could* see it, without being crazy, and even other people could, for example the landlord and the previous tenant, was nonetheless a figment of my subconscious. "You hear these strange stories," Bill had said. "A guy in Afghanistan kept seeing a black animal running through the compound at night, Several of the guys did. But there was no animal, not physically. It was their tension made manifest, the omnipresent watch for a faceless, barely-seen enemy – a Night Beast."

Neither he nor I ventured the opinion the headstone might surely indicate my own fear of death, or of its life-equivalent, societal obliteration.

I left that aspect of my problem with him, and we parted near Kensit Gardens. It was sunny, the trees in full leaf, pretty girls in shoe-lace shoulder-strap dresses, or low-slung jeans.

"You know," Bill confided, as the taxi he'd hailed sidled to the kerb, "it's almost a pity you've got this new job -I could have put something quite decent your way right now, only I never knew where to find you."

Then he was gone. As I stood there, stunned into a moronic inability to switch my own gears and shout *I lied* – what – *what* can you put my way – ?

Alone I took my long walk then. I supposed I could always look him up at the pub again. Tell him the truth. But probably he'd just been boasting, now I was safe and he didn't need to back up the promise. The best of us do that, don't we? I don't know why.

Just as I didn't know that when I got back, the Greyve would be lying on my bed.

I pulled up one of the chairs and sat down beside the bed. This was the pose of a friend or relative at the funeral couch of the sick. I squinted at the thing as it lay there, so silent and inert, supine, unhuman. Edward Grey.

Night arrived and blotted up the windows as night does now, in towns and cities, not with ink blue and drifts of distant stars, but with the runny orange jelly of streetlamps and the constant flash-lights of passing traffic. When these flashes came, the Greyve glowed wet-cold pink or white. Otherwise it was jelly-amber.

At some point I got up and put on the TV and made myself an instant coffee. But I didn't watch the first or drink the second.

I sat there, the only grieving carer of a dying stone.

There were no troubled reminiscences, pleas or accusations to listen to or try to soothe. No hand to hold. I didn't want to touch that smooth slick surface. I couldn't bring myself to, let alone to haul it off the bed. Let alone to lie down there in its place. Let alone to lie down beside it.

But my outing had tired me. I fell asleep. I woke about 4 a.m. to a stiff neck and some inane madhouse on the TV.

The Greyve still lay motionless, unmoved, but through the window the lamps were weak as watered orange juice and the sky was growing lightly flushed. *Day grew red...*
Dryad grew E.
Dad grew rye.
Deady grr we.
W rag red dye.

"Still got yer stone then?" merrily questioned the landlord that lunchtime, when I went into his lair for some chips.

"Uh – oh, yes."

"What's the name on it now?" I gaped at him. Helpfully, leaving the girl to splash on with the fryers, he popped out and stood too close to me, as he often does. "It had another name, see, with the other bloke. What was it?" He racked his three or four brain cells. "Woman's name?" he asked something vaguely. "*Millie* was it?" he mused, staring at my chips in their wrapper. "But your one says Eddy, yeah?"

"Edward," I spontaneously stupidly corrected, shifting the chips away from him – since he appeared likely to make a sudden impaling motion with his long sharp nose.

"That's right. Wasn't Edward, not before." He sounded disapproving. 'Millie' had been far nicer, it seemed. I decided to shore up my information.

"But the stone vanished when the previous tenant left, you said?"

"'S right. About a day before."

"Why did he leave?"

"What? How'd I know? Only know if I kicks them out. Guess he won the Lottery, yeah?"

A fruitless interval, I concluded, returning to the room.

The Greyve had still been on the bed, and still was when I went back in.

I sat by the window not looking at it, and ate the chips and drank some cold coffee left from the morning.

"What do you want me to do?" I had asked it, the Greyve, in the stony first light of new day.

Obviously I'd got, as ever, no reply.

The name on the Greyve changed this morning. That is I found it had, when I came in about 11 a.m., having stayed the night before at Bill and Susie's place, where even the guest apartment has an en suite bathroom.

I had the job interview too, yesterday. Two and a half hours. It seemed to go really well. Bill said later, from what he'd heard, I was in. So we celebrated. I stayed in shock mostly. Probably I still am in shock. I stood and looked round the room, even looked at the stone uncaringly, didn't take anything in. It seemed quite likely that inside a couple of weeks, unbelievably – *believably* – I'd be elsewhere. I'd be back in the golden *frame*. I'd be *myself* again.

Bill had set it up for me, of course. He had told me when he called me with the results of the Edward Grey word-searches, which everyone, he assured me, had enjoyed, some even (insanely) asking if Bill/I would let them know the final answer. In the middle of this welter of rubbish – "It may be phonetic even. For example, if you just *vocalise* the letters of the name Edward Grey – Ee dee double U etc: – you get a potential code that reads something like: Apostrophe E – that is, He – doubles you – that is, *can make two of you* – and *A hardy* – or *'ardy* – *horse is the reason why* – which may be a betting clue, possibly. I'll send you all the print-outs – there are *thirty* of them – by good old crawl mail, as you can't use your computer." And then, offhand and light, he added, "Oh, by the way... look – I took a chance – Do you want to check my new company out? I know for a fact they've looked at your past record, and would be happy to see you. And well, I mean, come on, it struck me – if your new outfit won't even give you a home lap-top – You're worth more than that, you know."

I suspected he hadn't credited a word I'd said after all, God bless him. Oh thank God he hadn't.

Once I could speak I told Bill I *would* like to come in and meet with his people in London. After we finished talking I sprawled in the chair by the window and cried for a minute. I'm not going to lie about this.

And then when I looked round, the Greyve was still there on the bed, and it still said *Edward Grey*.

But this morning, now I look properly, it says something else.

Still apparently a name. *Miles*. That is the first part of the new name.

I'm moving today. Not much to take with me. Everything is laid on ahead of me. A job. A car. A flat in a reasonably good area. Other possibilities, perhaps. Perhaps...

It's gone, the headstone. It got off the bed first, and I found it again stood in the corner. But I was already comfortably sleeping on the floor by then.

None of the Edward Grey ideas or anagrams or code-readings, or what-the-hell-else, made any sense, or where they did, no sense that seemed to relate to gravestones being in the room.

Naturally I ought to end this by saying that I heard later a guy called Edward Grey moved in after me and died quite soon, on the bed, (which wouldn't surprise me, the bed being the cripple-artist it is). But I think I never will hear that, and I'm unlikely ever to be in this neck of the urban woods again anyway, after this afternoon. While the name of course had, and stayed, changed, until the whole stone left the room, moving unseen as ever, while I slept. *Miles Tone.* That was the second name I saw on the Greyve. Milestone.

Bill had told me the episode originated in my subconscious, presumably also, then, in the id of the previous tenant, and that of any subsequent victim of this apparently benign and playful psychic practical joke.

In my case – maybe the last guy's too – it certainly seems to have been a friendly omen. Not a grave at all, though so like one in looks: instead a marker of the way, a destination – where? How many miles –

Maybe, as one of the other 'code-solutions' suggested, I should just add up the letters of the name – 10 – or the words – 2 – or the mystic numbers of the alphabet letters, where A is 1 and Z is 26 – applying them to the name, which would make an improbable 110. Or then again perhaps *Edward Grey* is a spelling mistake – Edmund Greg, possibly, or Edgar Green. It might be, after all, the error of some alien awareness that only meant to write GOOD LUCK! Or some curse concealed within the velvet marble glove.

My transport has arrived.

I glance about, past my few boxes and the single suitcase. Into the shadowy corners, across the bare lumpy mattress, at the cold and fissured walls.

Beyond, there's the future, and I'm ready.

We live with a thousand different deaths always and everywhere about us. But life doesn't have to be a cemetery.

I haul my stuff outside and lock the door. I'll drop the keys off at the chippy, as instructed. A minute more and I'll be in the taxi, driving west. In less than half an hour I'll have left it far behind, this segment of existence. The Greyve.

I shall write this down on the end of his notes. Then it may just seem silly.

I only found them, these notes, yesterday. Sorting things out at last. They made me sad, but I'm sad all the time, obviously. He only died three months ago, my husband.

We'd married immediately his divorce came through. We were together twelve years. What they say, wonderful years. I *liked* him. I loved him.

He was always very lucky, too. Everyone said that. All his business ventures went well. And no enemies. He was lovely. He always tried to be fair, said people had been fair to him. He always said too it was Bill who changed his luck, brought him "back from the grave", he used to say. And he and I met because I knew Susie, Bill's wife.

All the time though, I *never* knew my husband be whimsical, or *mystical* – so when I found *this*, written, presumably, when his luck changed after that earlier dark period, when he was forty-two, just before he moved – I was puzzled, at first. I wondered if it was a sort of short story he'd decided to write, for want of something better to do. I mean, it was fantasy fiction, Kafka-esque as he said, that stuff about a moving headstone – the *Greyve* – *Edward Grey* and *Miles Tone* – it even made me laugh for a few seconds, and I haven't laughed since he died. It was peaceful, thank God, his dying. In his sleep. A heart attack. We didn't know there was anything wrong. No symptoms, unless he just never mentioned them... They said it could have happened at any time. But it was the night after his fifty-sixth birthday. Too young – too bloody young nowadays to die – But I'm not going to start that again. He *did* die. He's dead.

So I told Bill about finding these notes or story or whatever. They were such friends, he wouldn't have minded me talking it over w i t h Bill. And Bill said h e 'd never seen any story, so I gave t h i s to him to read, and Bill said, "Yes, I *remember* t h i s – I mean it really did seem to happen to him – though truly I didn't know he'd taken notes –" and Bill laughed a bit too. And then his face went sort of set and grey. Oh God, play on words unintended. *Pale* then. He went pale. I said, Are you all right? And Bill said, "It's just – what he says here about the numerology system Mike worked out – when we were all trying to figure what that name – Edward Grey – might mean – i f it weren't just a name but a sort of code..." I asked, So what was it? Bill said slowly "Well, he didn't quite get what Mike meant, evidently. Because you don't run the numbers of the alphabet from 1 to 26, usually. Each letter still represents a number and then you add them all up. But they go in blocks of 9 – A to I – that's 1 to 9. Then J to R is 1 to 9 again. Then S to Z, which is 1 to 8." I see, I said, not seeing. And then Bill suddenly went red instead of pale, and he said "Sorry, I'm being a pedant. Come on. Let's go and find Susie and have a drink."

I could tell he didn't want to say anything else, thought he was probably upset, or he thought he might be upsetting me worse... Bill is so tactful. So I helped cover his sadness or his faux pas, whichever. And we all went out to lunch, as planned. But then, about halfway through the meal, this dreadful idea came to me that something about the numbers had somehow revealed to Bill that my husband had been involved with another woman during our married life together. Because Bill is brilliant at maths. He can add, multiply, sub-divide, whatever, in his head. To apply and add up numbers to a name would be instantaneous for him. He'd just *know* – So I said I was sorry but I felt a bit ill, and I got away and came back home. By which time the stupid idea of adultery had worn off. I *knew* my husband. He hadn't cheated. It wasn't that that turned Bill grey, then scarlet with a sort of terrified guilt of saying what must never be said.

Here in my now permanently empty house – we never wanted kids, and I'm glad I haven't got any, they wouldn't help – I sat in the twilight, the *grey* twilight, and I kept on thinking about working the alphabet as one to nine, one to nine, and one to eight: A to I, J to R, and then S to Z. And Bill's appalled face became stronger and stronger in my mind. And in the end I wrote down *Edward Grey*, and next what all those letters came to – E-5, D-4, W-5, A-1, R-9, D-4 – which made twenty-eight, and then, rather oddly, G-7, R-9, E-5, Y-7 – which also made twenty-eight. Finally I added together the two twenty-eights. Fifty-six.

Now I still sit here, though I've not turned any lights on and the garden trees hide the street lamps. It's really too dark to see the numbers any more. So maybe I made a mistake, and if I don't *look* again I can always assume later I *was* mistaken. I can assume that the luck-changing milestone of *Edward Grey* did *not* come with its built-in predicting proviso that my husband, thereafter, would only live fourteen years, till the night of his fifty-sixth birthday.

The Heart of Ice

A casual but fine piece of artwork by a friend, the very portrait of the beauty described at the tale's beginning, caused this story to evolve. Though unluckily the art couldn't be used as an illo in the black-and-white-only magazine that first published it. In a very odd way, I myself detect the influence of Hans Andersen, too. Less through the icy cruelty of his Snow Queen, than his crystalline snowscapes, the sense of otherwhere inextricably tangled in the everyday, and if loneliness — also self-collection.

Oh, the Ice Maiden. He has been hearing of her since he can remember. Her dark and coiling hair with the gleam in it of blue-green coal, her jewellery of icicles, her eyes that are like frost on lapis lazuli. But her skin is warm, the colour of honey, which from a distance can make her for an instant seem almost human. She dresses in the pale furs of winter beasts which she charms from their backs, leaving them naked but for shivery flesh and bones in the bitter cold. And then she clothes them instead in ice and they become ice-creatures, and her servants.

Nirsen worked in the town. He had been apprenticed at five years of age to the Kuldhoddr, who with his boys bought the unwanted things of the townspeople and hauled them to his yard, where they were sorted and turned into other things – such as broken pots into filling for wall-building, or spoilt furniture into firewood, or old garments into rags – and resold. Nirsen was by now nineteen and this was all the life he knew, the town life of buying, sorting, smashing, chopping, tearing, and so on. He knew the shabby house of the Kuldhoddr, where he slept in a shed off the yard with the other once-boy, now twenty, Jert. This one did not like Nirsen, had bullied him when they were children, and currently sneered and played adult tricks on him. The Kuldhoddr was himself a villain, and his wife a sow. The house, the work, the bad food, the winding narrow self-centred town, the whole of existence were foul to Nirsen. Even the red-cheeked girls that Jert leered after did not entice him.

Yet beyond the town lay the fields that in summer turned yellow, and in the winter black then white. Out there too lay the stretches of the river that were not choked with muck, but flowed in summer like, ale with strawberry fish in it that in winter froze themselves to pewter. Beyond, the great forest began, ash and birch and pine, and this ran all the way to the distant mountains, far as outer space. And the summer woods were green and the mountains lavender, but in winter both were white and the home of the Ice Maiden.

Where had he heard of her first? Nirsen could not recall, but he must have been a baby then, for it was before the Kuldhoddr bought him (one more thrown-out thing) and clobbered and smashed and thrashed him into a new, more useful article.

Even in the house of the Kuldhoddr, however, the Ice Maiden was spoken of, as a sort of curse – "May the Ysenmaddn take him and hang his skin on her trees!" Or whispered to by the wife as she stirred her filthy soups on the fire: "Don't you be harming my poor fingers, Lady Ice." For it was a fact the wife had had a finger bitten off by the frost one year, and everyone knew the Ice Maiden made the frost. It spun from her blue eyes and dropped from her mouth in her cold sweet breath, but changed to needles and knives in the air. It would paint the round windows prettily over, but if ever the Ysenmaddn caught you out of doors and you could not get away, she kissed you and froze you, and then her frost filmed over your eyes like the windows and blinded or crippled, or you were dead.

Amulets were put up to placate her on half the houses, though it was supposedly a Godly town. These were in the form of little man dolls all in a white spindly mummy-wrapping, like the rime, or they were polished awls, or the long teeth of wolves or foxes or the skull of a white cat or a white owl. She liked white animals best (if she took their coats she made them new ice ones that were whiter.)

Offerings, such as dead hares and round cakes were slung by the forest's edges or along the inner tracks, by hunters and wood-cutters. But few ventured into the trees once snow was down.

And now it was.

The russet town was muddy white, but the fields and forests and the mountains and the sky were whiter, like scrubbed china. And as they ran from smoky hot brazier to brazier at the corners of the streets, the children sang this rhyme:

Leave on our hands, Queen of Ice.
Leave on our feet, Queen of Ice.
Leave on our noses, Queen of Ice.
Yet take it all and leave us life –
Such a small price, such a small price.

One freezing night Nirsen went to the tavern on Killfox Street and drank a couple of cups. He spoke to no one, liking no one. As for the tavern girls he turned his face away, and then they called him names – High Nose, Little Cockerel. He had never been with any of them. They loathed him like an alien, as if he had two horns growing out of his head. But the drink was comforting.

When he got back he entered the yard beside the Kuldhoddr's house. The Kuldhoddr was away at the other end of the town, bargaining and drinking with some merchants. In the kitchen window smeared a tiny orange chink of light. Nirsen rapped softly on the door. The idea of the fire's embers appealed before he slunk to the shed.

When no one answered he slipped the latch.

Inside the kitchen, ah now. The sow wife was riding with Jert, and each of them grunted and moaned in pleasure. Nirsen felt sick, for he hated them both as they him, yet too they broke his heart, poor things, trying to find joy in the glacial heart of winter and unkindness. He would have gone away and said nothing.

But Jert on some sudden impulse turned from his work and learned he and the wife had been seen.

He shambled up, pulling his clothes together, his face already a clenched fist.

"You," was all he said. But the single word was a malediction.

Then he sprang and Nirsen fell back on the stone floor under the weight of him.

There they struggled, and in the background the dishevelled, nine-fingered woman babbled, and then she grew utterly quiet and a shadow splayed over the fighters which smelled of ale and said, "What's this?"

Both Jert and Nirsen were bloody but Nirsen had perhaps had the worst of it. He was lighter, and anyway Jert was accustomed to fighting.

It was Jert who rose and, with the wife whimpering behind him, he exclaimed, "She screamed out so I come running. He was at her, had her down, and Mrs trying to beat him off and calling for you. Hadn't I come in he'd have done her, your wife."

Nirsen lay stupidly marvelling at Jert's ingenuity, and heard the woman say, "It's true. Ruined I'd have been, you off at your business. But Jert was our friend and saved me."

After which the Kuldhoddr leaned right the way down to the kitchen floor, and he lifted Nirsen up from it with a curious sort of tenderness, all the time peering into his face. The Kuldhoddr did not ask what Nirsen had to say on any of this. Nor did the Kuldhoddr pass any comment. About a minute after he slammed his fist twice into Nirsen, at the heart and at the jaw, and everything collapsed in a storm of black pain and roaring.

When he came to, Nirsen did not know immediately where he was. He had been somewhere similar during the summer, for occasionally in the long fine evenings he would walk out to the edges of the fields, sit on the grass of the pasture and watch the fringes of the forest, where rabbits and squirrels and birds darted in the last westered sunlight. But he had never been out here in winter. Few ever were. It was another country now.

And in the land of full winter, here he lay, and much closer to the wood indeed. Over his very head arched the first deep ranks of the trees, the ash and birch with thick foliage of white snow, and the tall pines and firs beyond, crystallized. Glass beads and pipes and strands of ice had spun all the trees together too. The forest hung now inside the web of some giant ice-spider. Darkness was coming, the sky cold lead, and a thin wind whistled through the forest's avenues.

Nirsen understood well enough what had happened while he was helpless. He had been cast out for his supposed crime of attempted rape. There were stories of such punishments as this. No one would have minded. Why harbour the wicked when the winter would see to him?

He found they had bound his hands and his feet in case he should wake and struggle with them, but he had not woken till now. He shifted round to see and one of the cords on his wrists snapped. His hands were not well tied, both Jert and the Kuldhoddr would have been drunk. Besides, the cold made such cheap rope brittle.

Quite soon Nirsen was free. Then he stood up and looked back from the forest towards the town.

How small and murky it was under its huddle of dirty snow and smokes. The bleak fields between, white as starched tablecloths in rich houses, showed only the trample of the two men's feet and the snake-track of Nirsen's body as they had dragged him.

Without warning Nirsen found he had fallen down again. It came to him how hurt he was, also that he must have lain here most of one night and a day unconscious, for it had been before midnight when he reached the yard and now a second night was just starting.

Surely he should be dead? Perhaps he was. His face ached and gnawed where it was struck and his heart felt sometimes as if it stumbled. His hands were almost numb, the fingers too pale, threatening the awful frostbite. He could feel nothing of his feet – partly the reason he fell. He wore his outdoor clothes but they were not of course of the best. His head was uncovered.

He sat on the white earth under the white trees and the web of the giant spider, and knew if not yet dead still shortly he must be. But he could not go back to the town. Only the forest seemed to offer any shelter. At least it was a better place to perish, cleaner and far more beautiful.

Once again he rose and stamped about until, though no feeling came, yet his balance re-established. Presently he moved forward in among the trees.

Night arrived. The forest sank to dark silver.

As he trudged drearily onward, Nirsen heard the sound of darkness begin, the night chorus of owls and foxes, and once maybe a wolf, for in such weather wolf packs might well run this way. But there were stranger sounds also. He started to hear them and put them down to the sudden cracks of branches broken under the snow's weight; frozen streams that had fissured in the greater tepidity of day and now were sealing shut again; the wind, breathing. But really he knew what they were.

He was entering the kingdom of the Ice Maiden.

Those splinterings were the noise of her mirrors smashing; those murmurs like sealing ice were the resonance of draperies drifting over floors of snow. The clink and hush of the wind was an echo of some music played for her. And there! That sheer light platinum note – oh, that was the Maiden's laughter. Something had amused her tonight. Maybe it was the thought of one more lost outcast stumbling through her world, with Death treading close behind.

Nirsen continued until he could go no further. He was aware that to stop now meant that he must stop living. But finally another footstep became impossible. He took it but never moved. So then he slid down and leaned against the silver stalk of a tree, and watched the forest glowing though no moon had risen, shining from its own deathly whiteness, so the black sky changed to tin threaded with the blue sequins of stars.

But the blue stars were the eyes of the Ysenmaddn. Pitilessly they gazed at him, and yet it was not truly pitiless. How could one like she comprehend that his wretched little existence had been precious to him, or that to lose it was, for him, his greatest tragedy? Go to sleep, he imagined that she whispered through the snow-leaves. Go to sleep like a good child. And only a slight impatient indifference was in her voice. Nothing sinister or cruel. For she had no heart to be heartless with, the Ice Maiden.

An animal crouched over him. This now was what woke him up. He took it for a wolf – perhaps the very beast he had heard earlier in the night. But then his sore eyes, caked with rime, widened and Nirsen saw it was one of her creatures. It was a wolf of ice.

Whiter than any whiteness of the woods, it gleamed with the sleek pure sheen of steel. Every tuft of its pelt was sculpted from ice. Its mask-like face was ice, yet had both expression and potential ferocity, and the profound, solemn wolfish eyes gazed through, the unexpected colour of gold. And then it licked out across its glacial meltless mouth with a living tongue, and he saw its ivory teeth – all that, inside the skin of ice the Ysenmaddn had given it.

The beast will kill me, he thought. He woodenly composed himself, half dead as already he must be, to endure this finish as best he could

But the wolf only touched his cheek with its rock-hard freeze of muzzle, then raised its head. The howl raked the forest, the sky. The stars shook but did not fall.

Then the others drew near. Nirsen, in his deathly trance, watched. Not for an instant did he reckon he dreamed any of this. There were the two ermines, now ice-clad, their black markings caught perfect in the white slippery glitter of their coats. There was the albino bear, its thick fur all ice and ruffling and combing back and forth as it moved. Some ice-foxes came and played savagely before him as if to demonstrate that even when nipped or scratched their icy overlay was not disturbed. Ice-rats bustled from between the claws of tree roots and stared with chestnut eyes. Last the white owl floated down, silent as a single white feather, and settled on his boot, regarding him from its own round eyes which, in that moment, reminded him oddly of the pale lemon faces of two clocks that showed time had ceased.

Maybe he lapsed; it was like sleep but was it only death? Yet then once more he was woken and he was being dragged again, as his two human enemies had dragged him from the town. Now it was the wolf and the bear that pulled him, their taloned nails, their teeth, fastened in his clothing. The foxes pushed at him. The rats ran by and across him like overseers, and the ermines padded like bodyguards at his sides. The owl flew above them. He observed its metallic solidity passing along weightless just below the web of white quartz branches. Its wings hypnotized him: every feather chiselled from ice –

Nirsen sensed the earth under his body turning toward morning. He did not grasp what that could be, for he had had no education and did not know it was the earth which turned, as he had never seen that, only the sun rising or going down.

The bear it was who alone hauled him the last distance, bundling him across huge roots that slammed his spine like hammers, so this beating seemed far more brutal than anything Jert or the Kuldhoddr had done to him.

By then a sort of mist or smoke was lifting from the ground. It was like breath on a mirror, and through it the embroidered boughs of the great trees had been unstitched. A view opened. A lake spread before him. It was frozen to alabaster, save now and then you saw thinner places that dully glimmed. In the middle of the lake something rose up.

The bear dropped Nirsen. From behind, the wolf now was pushing at him. He found he had sat up.

The mist rippled and somewhere near a flower-pink stain was seeping: dawn sharpened the scene of the frozen lake, and so Nirsen saw the palace of the Ice Maiden standing at the lake's centre.

It was like a vast crystal goblet, and filled with a fizzing champagne light.

He thought, flatly, Well, I have seen it. It exists. Hadn't I come here I should have missed it. At least this I've done.

But then he glimpsed the sled of ice that had appeared on the lid of the lake, and how by itself it glided to the shore. The bear with a grumbling curdle of a growl rolled him over on to the sled. How cold the sled was, far colder than the snow. It seared him and he did not care. He would be dead before he reached the palace. Good, good, that was good.

There are chimes all through the house of the Ice Maiden. They depend from all the high, high walls under the wide sky, for here there is no roof. The snow never falls here, or if it does it becomes simply part of everything else – a curtain, a screen, a mosaic. But the chimes chime with a fearful tinsel deliciousness. It is like sucking raw icing-sugar to hear them. They please, but they sting.

There are no windows. The entire edifice is transparent. Any who are inside can always see out. Yet from the outside nothing can be seen within but for the lumination of the enormous chandeliers. These stretch from the roofless spaces above until they reach the floors that are perhaps a quarter of a mile below. Prisms and slender opal pillars comprise the chandeliers, and they convey a candleshine that has no candles, nor, night or day, do they go out.

These floors of the Ice Maiden are laid with circular tiles, each of which is the top of a human skull, remorselessly waxed and rubbed so slim it has become impervious and will magically carry any weight. Who – what – then rubbed them? The refining winter wind, who is never afraid of the prolonged harsh work of brooming, beating, scouring.

There are ice cisterns set in the bone floors where fish, scaled in ice, swim and frisk over little pebbles like polished zircons, which possibly they are.

Then the Ice Maiden comes in.

She is attended by invisible or partly visible beings that are wind-spirits, frothy flurries of light snow, or beasts which have died and become themselves bones, but that still want to remain with her never-theless.

She is as they say she is. Her skin is like honey, and from a reasonable way off she looks almost like a young mortal woman. Her hair is wavy and darkest blue – that might also seem pale black until you look carefully. She is crowned with a diadem of ice. Her garments are white fur. But her ears are like the ears of no human thing, more dainty, pointed, and she wears in them jewels of ice.

Her eyes. Her eyes define and defy everything ever said of them. You believe they may be dark until she looks at you. Then they are blue as lapis, just as all the legends tell, lapis lazuli behind sparkled casements of frost. And they are terrible. For they have no wickedness in them and know no malignity and no wish to deliver pain. But they know nothing of need, nothing of empathy, nothing of the merest momentary kindness, nothing like that. And they never will.

Nirsen has stood up on the floor of impervious skulls. Thinking he is dead now he feels strong and not unwell.

He bows to the Ice Maiden because he knows one must, with royalty, or they will be angry. But too he senses she feels no anger either. To bow is foolish, but he does.

She says nothing to him. Although he has been shown her eyes, if she even really glances at him he is unsure.

Does she credit he is here? Will it matter to her?

A boar that is made of bones nuzzles at her hand. She does nothing, does not respond, yet a mild flame runs through the skeleton of the beast. It is plainly happy and canters round and about, and all its vertebrae twinkle. Each of the others wants to touch her then, and she seems to allow this, for it happens.

Nirsen though would never dare attempt it.

He stands there and stares and listens to the chimes. Is he now her slave? He supposes she does not require slaves, requires nothing. Even the furs she steals he now suspects are not stolen. Probably they spontaneously fly off to adorn her and then she sighs her fragrant breath and never notices the animals reclad in living ice.

However, since she is there looking at him – or not – and being himself human and a man, in the end he speaks.

"What am I to do, Lady?"

The Ice Maiden answers.

Nirsen lowers his head.

Of course she has replied in her own language. He tries at once to retain and analyse what the words were like. Mostly, he thinks, like the sound of the chimes. He could not and does not understand and doubts he will ever have the means to learn.

Again he speaks. "I'm lost then."

At this, strangely, the faintest glint of something crosses through her gem-stone eyes. But she has no humour, he believes, as no cruelty or compassion. Surely, despite his notion in the forest, she could not be amused.

Besides anyway, this is when she moves on over the long floor between the stalagmite-stalactite chandeliers, her crowd of insubstantial attendants furling round her like a fog. She vanishes somewhere amid the curtains of frost.

Just then Nirsen realizes he has regained total feeling in his feet and hands and ears. His throat is moist and does not hurt, the ache in his face has gone. He has, apparently, eaten and drunk, and he is warm. This must be because he is dead, then. But no. Strong and bravely now his heart is beating in his chest.

He goes to the curving side of the glass of the palace and stares out.

He sees the long lake and the tangle of the archetypal forest all around. The sky is golden as the eyes of the ice-wolf. When he puts one finger to the palace glass it gives off a delicate note, as a refined goblet would if tapped, say, with a priceless ring.

There is no way out – or in – that he can detect.

If he is a prisoner he doubts, but nor does he have liberty. He checks every so often to be sure he has not become all bones, or is sheathed in ice, like the animals here. But he is only as he always was, there in his growing beard, and his poor clothes that do not suit the palace (as his beard does not) and his whole skin with his heart thumping rudely and healthily away.

After some hours during which he wanders through the veils and partitions of the seemingly endless chambers, he sits again on the skull floor to look out of the window which is wall. Time does seem to have passed in the normal manner, for now it is evening. A flight of winter swans flies over, real birds whose white is plumage not ice.

The sun sets like a red wound, except now he knows it does not set at all. Instead the earth turns backward, away from it. In the cisterns the glistening fish weave patterns and at last he sees they do not swim in water but in liquid silver. Now this scarcely matters. Night enters the palace and the chandeliers burn no more brightly. Spirits appear to shimmer through the air. An owl of flesh and feathers perches high up on the rim of the tall goblet and calls once in its voice like a ghost, before flying away. Can Nirsen sleep? He will try. Ah yes, thank God, he can.

How often does he see the Ice Maiden after that? Does he count? Yes, but then forgets. He forgets.

How can you remember anyway such a visitation? It would be as if a man said I will count up every occasion I see that star appear in the sky.

Sometimes she does seem to pause, and to examine Nirsen for a while. Then, as the days and nights continue, he wonders if he can ask her for something, as in stories the woebegone man does ask the supernatural being to grant his heart's desire. But Nirsen has been trained only in sorting and demolishing rubbish into greater dross. He has learned to have no heart's desire, cannot imagine one. Or else he has simply been too wise to harbour dreams.

Only one more time does he try to talk to her. He says, tentative, "Here then am I, but why then I, not others?"

And as before she seems to reply. But in her own language like chimes and little bells, and ice that deliberately splinters.

Besides, he knows he is alive. His body works almost completely, breathing and letting him see and think and walk or sit, and even sleep. He needs no food or drink, and therefore the other accessory functions to do with digestion do not trouble him either. He is warm. Really it would be an imposition to petition the Ice Maiden for any other thing, particularly an explanation. So then he asks no more, only bows to her and steps aside if she enters a part of her palace where he has taken himself. But frequently, too, she passes high up in the air, moving some way off over the floorless space between the upper tines of the chandeliers, the snow and spirits and skeletal animals dancing round her, affectionate and undemanding.

It reminds him a little of some priest's view of God's Heaven. He had never credited that; it had sounded also boring to Nirsen, for he was used to having to work despite the low and ugly nature of his labour. He is not bored in the palace, however, though he has nothing to do. Indeed he does do something, which is that he goes from area to area of it, and he watches the world outside, that is the abbreviated region of lake and encircling forest, and the sky.

In these he finds astonishing constant metamorphoses. They are like books he can read. He studies all the ways that snow comes, and slight thaws, and dawn and day and sunfall, dusk and night, and clouds, and all the stars and planets, and the moon and sun. The lives of the outer animals that survive he is a student of, and also he sees how two die, one a deer and one a hare, there by the lake's margin. But a while after he notices that the blithe and lively skeletons of a deer and a hare have added themselves to the Ice Maiden's entourage. This puzzles him slightly. So many creatures die in winter, seen or unseen, surely there should be more about her. But then it occurs to him not all the dead would want to come to her. Then the other persistent riddle is sharpened, as to how it is he is here alive. Again, despite all evidence, he wonders if he is.

Whatever else Nirsen, doubting or indifferent, goes on with his scrutiny of the outer world. On certain nights he is so immersed in it he forgets to sleep.

But then there is a night when he does slumber and at daybreak he is wakened by a dreadful noise.

He starts up thinking that at last his heart has cracked in two pieces. But it is the lake that has cracked in twain. Black water bubbles up.

Nirsen notices how the edges of the forest are dripping white, cool tears.

In a day or so colossal ledges of snow slide crashing from the trees. Through a shallow place in the lake he catches sight of iceless bluish fish, swimming and rising to a narrow slot where all the frozen lid has gone. On the boughs above, a fearful reddish glint begins to show like fire during the afternoons. Spring is returning.

That evening a bird of bone, perhaps once a sparrow, flies down through the air layers of the Ice Maiden's palace, and sitting on Nirsen's shoulder it twitters in the startling bird-language of the outer world. Is it warning him? He thinks that it is.

Had he a bag he would pack it. He would be ready. He longs to see her one further time, but she does not appear, and by the hour the moon – no longer white, but having a brazen face – crests the trees, the sparrow has flown away. Not upward among the chandeliers, but out through a tiny flaw in the goblet of the palace.

Nirsen does not risk sleep.

He waits, standing on the floor of skulls.

When the wild crunching and crackling begins he is not surprised. It is grief he feels. As if he must truly die now, or worse, for a fact, be born.

As the walls liquefy and pour in the melting lake, sailing from him in rafts like narrow pearl, the sled is there and he steps on it. It draws him away and away towards the shore.

He stares back. Every bit of the towering crystal of the palace has disappeared.

Of course, where could she go in spring?

Only slowly, as he nears the forest edge, does Nirsen recall the sparrow and wonder if, in the warm weather, the Ice Maiden emerges on to the earth in a different form.

Who then, what then, is she? Is she spring now? Summer next? He cannot understand. Landing on the muddy shore he observes the sled dissolve. The trees are flitting with birds and somewhere in the forest a stag bellows. Like beads small flowers decorate the ground.

Nirsen went away from the lake and, although he did not properly comprehend it, towards the town from which he had been cast out.

He knew no other place to go. It was instinct, or thoughtlessness.

As he trekked through the green lace architraves of the forest, he wondered where the ice-creatures took themselves in warmer weather. Did their pelts thaw too, and proper pelt grow back? Or did they melt altogether, and were there unseen streams of fox and bear, wolf, rat, weasel, owl, under his weary boots?

He hoped not to see their animal masks when he caught his own image in some puddle, nor did he. He looked as ever, but he had never had much interest in himself. The springing leaves spoke in a foreign tongue. Already they discussed him, whispering.

He dreamed of her when he sheltered by night. When he slept between the paws of tree roots or in skull caves beneath canopies of spreading fern. He saw again her amber skin and her icicle eyes. He was no longer frightened of her, if ever he had been. He felt a sort of cold love, but it was not entirely cold, nor love: it had no name.

Six days, five nights before he reached the fields where they were now sowing, and beyond them the huddle-muddle of the town.

How warm the spring was; the fields steamed. As if under the winter smoke the town was shrouded by vapour. He felt time had played tricks on him. He debated whether, as in old tales, he would find the town a hundred years younger than he had left it – or aged five hundred years into a future he could not know.

But reality is sometimes more unusual than myth.

Once in the town, considering events with greater prudence, he was wary, expecting threats or even a further assault. But those that looked at him seemed only suspicious. This struck him more and more as peculiar. They would, reasonably, reckon him dead.

Then a carter halted his load and strode over. "What you at here, stranger?"

Nirsen recalled him. The Kuldhoddr had several times bought things off the man with Nirsen waiting by. The town was not large. Everyone knew everyone to some extent. But not, it seemed, any longer Nirsen. For having muttered something appeasing to the carter and gone on, other similar inquiries came Nirsen's way.

At length, driven, he even sought the gate by the Kuldhoddr's yard – then shrank back as Jert burst suddenly out. But Jert glanced at and passed Nirsen with just a contemptuous thrust and cursing, "Get from the way!"

Nirsen had seen himself in water on the wet earth, and since entering the town in a window or two. He looked as he had always done.

He wandered through the town and out its other side.

On the track beyond he hesitated, considering. The sun punched down a furnace heat yet he did not sweat. The town too had been like a furnace. The breath of the people there had spooled like fog and had smelled of boiling water or cooking meat to him. Here on the track Nirsen found too something had burnt him on the arm. Lifting back his sleeve he saw a great blistering welt as if from a scorch or scald. It was where Jert's hand had pushed him.

There was pasture ahead with some goats.

As Nirsen travelled on, the animals turned one and all to watch him by. Even from the goats waves of heat emanated, and the tang of smouldering grass.

He trudged all day, away from the town and up into some low hills where the ringing hammer blows of the sun on his head were less bearable, but the landscape was empty of human habitation, and therefore of human incandescence.

When night fell he hoped for coolness, but there was not much difference. A full moon rose yellow and blazing, and he sheltered from its fire.

Through the soles of his boots the ground, in sunlight or darkness, flamed against his feet. If he should brush against a tree or shrub, he felt a surge as if warm steam pressed through his clothing. But when after some further days he went by a single hillside cottage, the heat that gushed from it was like dragon's breath. He had to know, and so set one finger's tip to the wall. It did not blister his skin as Jert's touch had done, yet it burned. It was like a pan just off the stove.

For days and nights again Nirsen went on. The spring was flowering into early summer. The heat of the sun and of most things reached a powerful crescendo, extreme and omnipresent. He could not bear it, but then he could. As with so many bad conditions, he grew used to it. Yet where able, he touched nothing with his unprotected skin. Even the coldest streams that ran down from the circling mountains, still fretted by the recent memory of snow, were tepid if he tried them. But he never drank from them, he did not feel thirsty ever, never hungry. He walked, and studied the book of the world. He was not distressed. Nor in any way exalted. In his life always it had been that he had little or less and must additionally put up with diverse troubles. Nothing had altered for him in that way then, though everything else had changed utterly.

Inevitably he was drawn back sooner or later to the forests. The far-as-space mountains were all that lay beyond and he sensed they, though not of man's making, would be torrid as the lava that once had seethed inside them. They were nearer to God too, presumably, being higher up, and certainly nearer the sun. These features must ensure they were, for Nirsen, killing hot.

Deep in the summer woods he discovered a rock cave. Chill moss smoked with warmth above an icy little stream softly warm as a bath. Here Nirsen took up residence.

Throughout the season he observed the plants and animals. He would sit all day, all night, as he had done on the skull floor of the Ysenmaddn, reading from the forest's pages.

Autumn-fall transmuted the metal of the woods to copper and bronze, and then the cold blew in wild sweet breaths. As the pines put on their white armour, of course he thought of the wide table of the lake. He thought of the palace of glass. He would never seek it save in his mind. He could no more return there than into yesterday.

But as the winter gathered, for Nirsen true spring had come, the time of plenty and of ease.

There in his hollow Nirsen lived a long, long life. He seldom stirred from his place, not needing to. Perhaps instead the beasts of the forest, undisturbed by his immobility, carried on their own existences not an arm's reach from him. Perhaps in the core of winter even the ice-beasts came, her creatures, to prowl around the cave, to lick his fingers with pliable cold tongues, to show him things or tell him things, for maybe he learned their language after all of necessity, just as he had, that way, once learned his own. Did the skeleton sparrow sit on a bough, or on his shoulder, and twitter to him and teach him also the secret tongue of birds and bones?

For sure, he never saw her again, the Ice Maiden, save in dreams and thoughts.

But two others saw her once, for the briefest moment, many decades later, and that was because of Nirsen.

It was summer by then, yet some hundred years or more from Nirsen's youth. The two fellows who forged through the forest were not oppressed by the sun at all; they liked it and boasted of it, as if they themselves had invented it, lit it and hung it up on a string to please the world.

But it was a hot enough day, and coming to a shady spot where a stream trickled from a cave, they sat down to eat their midday snack.

"That tree there," said one, pointing with his knife, "that we'll have over for the merchant's fancy door."

They were wood-cutters, sizing up the woods to choose things to slaughter for the use of their town.

The other grunted. But then he said, "That cave-hole there, that's gloomy-chill enough. We might find some rare, tasty fungus along in there for the stew."

So when they had eaten, they got up and went over the bank and stood gawping in at the cave.

Cold enough? Oh yes. The cave was very cold. It was a hole back into winter, black and shining with the mail-coat of ancient ice, and spears and daggers of ice pointing downward from its ceiling, dense as iron. Even the stream was frozen over, only thawing once it had escaped the cave.

"I never saw summer such like that," said the older woodsman, "in all my born days."

"Look there," said the other hoarsely, "what's that?"

The bolder older man went in. He leaned forward and beheld a heap of human bones and a human skull sat on top of them. He was not afraid of the dead. He did not understand what dead was, and that it might affect him ever seemed unlikely. And so peering shamelessly through the bones he saw another thing, and, curious, he bent to pick it up. "See here this lying in the middle. It's a chunk of slate, and a picture on it."

But the other would not go in, and then the old man drew the lump of slate from among the toppled bones and brought it outside, into the sunshine.

That way both men saw the picture fashioned on the slate. This was of a beautiful young woman with dark, bluish-greenish locks of hair, and a honey skin, and azure lips, and eyes like the blue icy shadows that gleam behind the face of the winter moon. By this era the stories of an Ice Maiden had been forgotten, or had chameleonized into some other legend, and the wood-cutters did not know what they saw. And it was only for a second anyway that they had the chance to look at it. For abruptly the old wood-cutter let out a yelp and dropped the slate, on which the image of the Ice Maiden was imprinted, down on the earth, where it shattered in a thousand fragments. "So cold – cold as the frost and ice it burnt me –"

And muttering oaths and prayers they hurried away, even sparing the tree they had meant to fell. The older man's hand would carry the scar to the day of his death. But the shattered slate had not been slate.

It was Nirsen's heart.

Calinnen

Like several of my pieces, including whole novels, I simply begin to write, atmosphere my only guide, and knowing nothing much about the protagonist, nothing at all of where we are heading. But I learned, I learned.

As Calinnen was riding back from the northern war, he saw a woman in a green gown standing by the track. Her hair was pale as lint, her eyes grey as the rain; she was much younger than the day.

"Sir," she called to him, as the horse drew level, "are you from the battle-place?"

"Yes. And now I am going home."

She lowered her eyes. Due to their colour, and the downpour, he could not be certain if she wept – or did not.

"Some there are," she said, "who never will come home from there."

"True," he answered coldly. "One of these was my brother. My tidings ride pillion behind me, heavier than my arms and armour."

"I regret your trouble," she said. "But I must ask you, do you know anything of the fate of one named Calinnen?"

Calinnen started. His name was not very common. How odd and unlucky-sounding this, that the woman should inquire of him after his namesake, that man probably being dead, for most were returned by now; he himself was one of the last.

"I have heard the name," he told her, with hidden irony. "No more than that can I vouch for."

"Alas," she said "Alas." And turning instantly away she went back among the trees that fringed the road.

Disturbed and peculiarly alert, he sat the horse and watched as she climbed the slope of the wood, and vanished into its shadows above. He thought to make out a stone house there, but was unsure. It was late summer, and all the trees in full leaf, and the rain too made it difficult to confirm. Nor did he think any accompanied her, either to wait on her or guard her. Perhaps she had lost everyone.

At this point he was, he had reckoned, only two days journey from his own estate. It was true he had not ridden this particular track before, since going out he had travelled with the king's army, on wider roads. He did not want now to lose either his time or his way, for in another hour or so the sun would set. He touched his horse's neck. They rode on.

The estate was in a poor condition. Many of the men who had worked it were, of course, dead in the war. Others, who had run away, did not now venture back. Calinnen's wife and his steward had held the place together as best they might. Calinnen's old father, a frail beetle, was little use for anything, and besides Calinnen had the awful news to tell him. To his horror and distressed relief, Calinnen's father seemed not to take in the fact of his second son's death. "Ah, there," he said, in a sad, pitying tone, "poor lad." And then, "We are to have a roast boar at the dinner. Why should that be?"

"I think they do it to welcome me," Calinnen said quietly.

"Ah, good, good. This is good."

That night Calinnen and his wife wept together, and later they were lovers. Both had remained faithful, or they had after a reasonable fashion. He guessed she had spent a little time with his steward, but their acts were discrete. Calinnen had naturally, now and then, availed himself of women on the march. Neither spoke of these things. Near dawn he roused from a broken sleep to hear her murmur, "I wish I might bear you a son, my lord." But she was barren; they both knew this, though did not discuss it.

Despite that he lapsed into a sort of dream, and dreamt that after all she was with child of him, and bore it, and it was a boy. And they named this son with his own name, Calinnen. And in twenty more years, when he, Calinnen himself, was dead, the youth fought in another of the king's wars and was slain. And in the woods two days from his lands, his young mistress waited in a green gown, and sometimes ventured to the road to ask of returning warriors: "Do you know anything of the fate of one named Calinnen?"

When he woke fully at sunrise, Calinnen found this dream stupidly haunted him. He took his wife aside and said to her, "If ever it happens I am gone and yet you bear me a son, never name him after me. Every man should have his own distinct name, so I believe." She nodded, but looked at him a while, silently. She did not remember what she had murmured in the dark before dawn, and perhaps asked herself if he now reprimanded her for her barrenness, or even her infidelity, as he never had in the past.

Days and nights elapsed, and he saw to the business of his house and land, but thoughts of the war still came to him. Sometimes he had terrible dreams. But he spoke of neither, and pushed them from him.

War was an evil essential of the world, yet one more of the curses brought down on Man by his earliest disobedience. It must be endured, and where necessary embraced, never invited back, as some men did, like a friend of long-standing, to the hearth of his mind.

One day, when he asked the old father how he did, the ancient man said sombrely, "I mourn for my son. He died in the war." This surprised Calinnen slightly, for until then he had been unconvinced his father grasped the tragedy. But that night Calinnen dreamed it was his brother and not himself who had ridden home and, in tears, told the household that Calinnen had perished in battle. While in the woodland two days from the house, a witch in a green gown had warned men that Calinnen's ghost was also on the road, mounted on a phantom horse, for neither of them knew that they had died.

Waking from this dream, Calinnen felt of his hands and arms and face. Getting up he examined his whole body, even staring at himself finally in his wife's mirror of Eastern glass. "Am I much changed?" he said to her. She shook her head, but he saw in that moment she thought him older, and less strong.

Calinnen now began to dwell, not on the war, but on the woman in green he had encountered.

He found it hard to shift her from his inner eye. And, too, he began to dream of her often. In these dreams nothing much happened, it was only that he saw her there over and over, by the track, in the falling rain that was like her eyes.

Had she been some witch? If so, he should go back and see what she was at, for maybe she had put a hex upon him. He felt always misplaced now, tired and uneasy, and no new thing, let alone any old one, gave him pleasure.

There came a day when it was not unsuitable he should go.

He told his wife and the steward he had a promise to keep, an old comrade he must visit to the north. He should be gone only four or five days. No one questioned this. It seemed to him his wife and the steward certainly would not miss him.

The year was turning, and the woods when he came in among them were a dreary sallow yellow, and the leaves fell always down like a reminder of dying.

On the first night of the journey, when he sheltered at a small ruined chapel, the dream he had was unlike all the others, although the woman again was in it.

During the dream he had at first been required to search for her, since the stone house he thought he had glimpsed up the slope did not exist. In the end he found a house made of mirror glass, which was almost impossible to discover, as it reflected all the wood back into itself. But a magpie flew over, reflected also, and perched on the roof, and that way Calinnen saw through the deception.

He knocked on the mirror door, where his own image now showed. The door smashed in pieces, and so therefore did his image.

Within, three women waited in a line. Their hair was pale as lint, their eyes not grey, but yellow as the fox-eye colour of the dying leaves. It was she three times over.

"Sir," they said, as one, "do you come here to have your doom retold? You know it well."

"You lie," he said. "What doom is that? I survived the battle. I am alive."

Then only the first woman spoke. She said: "Your doom is threefold. First of your doom is that your wife does not love you."

The second spoke next. She said: "Second of your doom is that you have no son to follow you."

The third spoke – and at this he raised his hand to stay her, but it was too late. She said: "Third of your doom is that you did not die."

"Poor man, you are alive," they said, all three together. "Alas, alas."

Calinnen woke, and drew his sword in the darkness. It was still sharp. She was a witch and he would kill her.

On the following night he only dreamed of the battle, and how he had almost been slain, yet the hail of blades and axes missed him; but then he found his brother, handsome and kind, and younger than he, hacked to scarlet on the earth.

It was an hour after sunrise when he reached the place on the track where she had waited. Now the sun slanted a different way. He saw at once, very clearly, all up the slope to where stood a building of stone.

He rode past two gates which hung wide and, dismounting, thundered his fist on the wooden door.

Presently a servant came.

"Where is your lady? She with the white hair."

The man's eyes widened, and Calinnen thought he would say: Oh, she is dead these twenty years, but her spectre haunts the road and curses men.

Instead the servant took Calinnen into a hall, and there left him. After a little the woman came, white-haired and grey-eyed, but on this occasion a tall man walked beside her.

Other things were changed also, for she wore today a red gown not a green one. And she smiled and was happy.

It was the man who asked him, cordially enough, what he wanted.

"I would have a word with her," said Calinnen. "She spoke to me some months ago, as I rode home from the war. She inquired of me if I had heard of, and knew the fate of another particular man."

"That was I," said the other man, and he too smiled at Calinnen. "She was part mad with fear for me, and would stray out to the road. Is this not so, my love?" he added, turning to her gently.

With a calm dignity she replied, speaking equally to him, and to Calinnen, "I do not deny it. Mad I was. But one evening as I waited there, I saw at last my beloved husband riding home, and in the instant sanity came back to me with my Joy. Here he stands now. But you, sir, are most generous to have returned to learn my fate and his."

Calinnen assumed then that they, in their mutual gladness, mistook his purpose. But even though he put on a civilized face for them, his disquiet and rancour did not go away. He spoke to the man at her side.

"It is of interest to me," said Calinnen, "that you and I, sir, bear the same name."

"Ah, do we so?" asked the man. And the woman laughed as a child does, pleased at life's sweet absurdity, its charity and hopefulness.

But Calinnen could not slough his anger. Harshly he said to

them, "How was it then that my name of Calinnen was given also to you?"

At this a pause came on the hall. A shadow fell there too, some taller tree perhaps that hid the progress of the sun.

"That is not," said the other man, "my name."

"No, nor is it," said the woman. "My lord is called Cadran. And so I asked all who passed if they knew anything of the fate of one so named."

"Calinnen was the name you spoke to me," he said.

"Cadran was the name I spoke. The name of my angel husband. Maddened I might be, but that I would not forget."

And the man came to Calinnen and mildly drew him back across the hall, where one or two other armed men stood watching them, until they reached the outer door.

"How could I mistake –" Calinnen asked, weary at last.

"It is easy done. Some fever in the ears. The sough of the wind perhaps, or falling rain. Farewell. May you be blessed. Do not return here ever."

Then through the weeping woods, over the neglected lands, to the spoiled estate, and desert of a wife, a sneering steward, a cobweb father, and the dark, rode Calinnen, knowing not any answer at all, or *knowing* all, all and too much. And night after night he dreamed of nothing. Not of the woman, or of his son or his brother, nor even of the battle. Of nothing, Calinnen dreamed, of nameless nothingness.

En Forêt Noire

At school, in the 1920's, my mother was taught (among many terrific things, all of which — including a library of faultless literature and maths — she retained till the end of her life) a little song from France. She recalled all the words, and the melody. And I, happy magpie that I am, stored references to the song in my 1981 werewolf novel Lycanthia. En Forét Noire je vais les soirs, part of the song began... 'Into the dark forest I go in the evenings'. Years after, John Kaiine suggested a scenario to do with a very dark forest. The plot was compelling, and quickly established itself with cast, actions and denouement. The title, of course, had only been waiting.

While the carriage was trundling towards the small city of Arlin, through the dusty summer fields – that was when Louis Corbière first saw it. The forest.

"What's there?" It was not Louis, but the fat lawyer travelling with his thin wife, who inquired.

Only one person, the wrinkled little clerk, knew.

"The Forest of Arlinacque. An ancient wood, said to have existed since the era of Charlemagne."

"Impossible!" exclaimed the lawyer, who, despite his question, believed he knew everything.

And the clerk said no more.

Later, at dinner in the inn on the Arlin Road, Louis
mentioned the forest to the innkeeper.

"That place. Oh, monsieur. It's too close for my comfort."

"Close? But it lies – what? – ten miles away from your inn here."

"Too close. I said."

"Why?"

"A bad spot, monsieur. Rotten. Dark in more than darkness."

Louis pondered, as he ate the roast meat and drank the wine. The Forest of Arlinacque had indeed looked very dark. Even in the blistering scorch of the late afternoon sun, it was entirely black in form, impenetrable. Huge pines, monumental yews, and other conifers, tangled together, were reaching high up into the thick, hot air. It had taken the coach, travelling quite fast, half an hour or more to pass the trees. But though Louis had striven to squint between them, he had seen very little. The aisles of the forest were like caves full of shadows. Beyond, the fields resumed, and beyond them, the hills, and finally the shape of the mountains was scratched out thinly on the sky.

Reverie ceased. The inn was generally rather noisy, seeming packed with soldiers, and shouting drinkers.

As Louis was retiring for the night, a stooped and very elderly and eccentrically old-fashioned man approached him on the inn stair.

"I heard you ask about the forest, monsieur. Perhaps you would care to glance in this book, which carries the legends of many areas, including that of Arlinacque."

"You're too kind."

The old man smiled and said, "I'm merely old, monsieur, and have been so for a long time. The only real pleasures left to me are to be either very kind, or very cruel."

Louis was young, not yet twenty-two, and old age was like another country to him. He felt sorry for its inhabitants. After all, life was dangerous and uncertain; he might never have to enter the country of the old.

Upstairs, he lit extra candles, and sat propped high in bed, reading the book the old man had given him.

It was, like the donor, an antique, published, it seemed, around the time of Louis XIII. As the Bourbon namesake turned the pages, ordinary Louis Corbière found fascinating anecdotes of ghosts, undines, dragons in hidden valleys, beautiful women imprisoned beneath ruined castles, and so on. Eventually he located a reference to Arlinacque. By then the candles were burning low, and he was tired. The ornamented print fluttered against his eyes, and before he had read more than five or six lines, he fell asleep.

Even so, the idea of the forest stayed with him, and followed him down into unconsciousness.

Louis dreamed he ran between dark trees, in darkness. Somewhere high above, a moon shone, flashing through pine-needles and branches like a silver sword. Ahead lay no safety – and behind was *terror*. Race as he might, he could not outrun the awful unknown horror which pursued him. His only hope would be to find a way out of the forest. And he had no chance of that, he thought, none at all.

He woke near dawn, sweating, his feet and fists stinging, because he had clenched them so hard.

Presently he laughed at himself. He was a grown man, on the way to visit his betrothed, for the first time in her family home. She was a pretty girl, who liked him. How foolish to succumb to childish fears.

In the morning, he bore the book, the passage on the forest unread, down into the main room of the inn. The elderly guest who had loaned it was nowhere to be seen – apparently not yet risen from his bed. Louis therefore left the book in the guardianship of the innkeeper, whose puzzlement might be a cover for intended theft. But Louis could do nothing else. The coach was due to leave in ten more minutes.

Dinner the next night was a quite different affair. Célie's parents, the de Lejays, had welcomed Louis, just as they had in Paris, bemoaned as usual his lack of a servant to travel with and take care of him, and presented him, laughing, to their blushing daughter. The afternoon progressed happily enough, through a rose-hung garden, to a pleasant enough evening, during which endless visitors arrived to greet Louis, culminating in a lavish supper. The table was swagged in lace, jewelled by candles and the best china and crystal, elegant, if often chipped. Sixteen people sat down to dine. Unfortunately one of them was Célie's brother. Marcellin.

Marcellin had never cared for Louis, or the betrothal, and made this plain in various 'playful' ways – as if only joking with Louis, rather than trying to catch him out or demean him. Louis' father had formed his wealth in trade, and so ably that Louis himself had not been required to enter the business, and instead had pretentions to study. The de Lejays meanwhile kept up minor aristocratic habits, but had fallen on hard – that was *moneyless* – times. Hence the match, with which everybody, saving Marcellin, seemed well-pleased.

"And how do you find the country, hereabouts?" asked Marcellin sneeringly of Louis, across the festive candles.

"Countrified," said Louis, smiling.

Célie's father laughed, and so did Célie, but Marcellin continued, "Come, come, Monsieur Louis. Surely you made out some difference between our region and the tame rambles around Paris? Or can you really not tell a hawk from a handsaw?"

Louis said, "Even Hamlet could do that, apparently, when the wind was blowing the right way."

"Oh, bravo. I'd forgotten you were a scholar. You must be," Marcellin added, "to go bouncing about in a public carriage without your servant."

Madame de Lejay raised her hands in alarm. Louis said, mildly, "I prefer to travel that way. And on journeys, servants get underfoot, I find."

"Then you should train them otherwise, monsieur. My Jeannot is *never* under my feet. He knows too well what I'd do to him if he got in my way."

Louis mentally considered Marcellin's Jeannot a moment, a villainous, leering fellow, with a scar across his forehead which, supposedly, Marcellin had given him years before.

Louis decided to change the subject. "I did see one thing that interested me greatly, as we drove here. A huge black forest of pine trees, that someone told me is called Arlinacque."

Madame de Lejay gasped, and crossed herself. A number of others at the table looked nervous.

"I beg your pardon," said Louis. "But – is it truly such a terrible place?"

"One never knows," said Monsieur de Lejay. He added sombrely, "A great many people have vanished there."

"Oh, worse than that!" cried a blonde lady across the table, who was a cousin of Madame's. "Men walk into that forest – and never come out of it. They are never seen again -nor any who go there to search for them."

"There is the story of a soldier," said Monsieur de Lejay, now even more heavily. "This happened only a few years back. He was seeking employment, having been wounded in the Prussian War, and was on foot, having given his horse for his debts. So he took an unfamiliar track to Arlin, and happened across the edges of the forest. An old woman was out on a field nearby, hurrying to get home in the dusk. But she ran over to him and clutched his arm. 'Don't go into the wood,' she said to the soldier. 'Why's that, Granny?' he asked her. She said that none who went in there ever came out again. Things were there, inside. Dreadful things, that sucked away blood and bone, and left only ashes blowing on the ground."

Louis glanced about him. What theatre! No one seemed to breathe. Even Marcellin looked uneasy, his eyes fixed on his father. Yet Louis himself, amused though he attempted to be, felt abruptly a sinking at his heart. He told himself it was nothing, and that he was too sophisticated to be made afraid by this provincial telling of horror-tales.

Monsieur de Lejay, however, went inexorably on.

"The soldier told the old woman, as others reported later, that he would heed her warning, but obviously he did that only to restore her calm. He had no intention of tramping all the way round the forest in order to avoid going into it, looking for the Arlin Road. He was already footsore, and perhaps thought very likely he would meet gypsies in the wood, or charcoal-burners, who might keep him company, and share some wine with him, through the night. So, soon after, he set off into the trees."

Monsieur paused.

"And then?" demanded one of the other relatives, a young lady with curls, who maybe had never heard this story before.

"And then – nothing, I fear. He went into the wood and, like the rest, never emerged from it. Although some persons from a nearby village, who were out on the pastures above, heard, during the night, hideous screams coming from among the pines. Such things had been heard before. They did not dare go to look. Then, in the days following, six of the soldier's companions from the war, discovering their comrade had vanished, went also to the Forest of Arlinacque – and one of these men *returned*."

Louis said, "But, monsieur, forgive me, I thought you said no one ever did."

"Ah, my dear friend. This young soldier had not gone *into* the forest, only to the very edge of it, from where he watched his brothers walk away through the trees. It seems he, too, had a wound, a sword-cut to the leg, and had sat down to rest, meaning after a minute to catch them up. But instead, as he told it, a fearful coldness and lethargy swept over him, almost a stupor, so he thought he would faint. And then it came to him how no sound was in the forest, not the rustle of an animal passing through, not the rattle of a bird's wings, nor any song or call. A silence was there and a darkness was there – and his companions were in the midst of it – but in that very moment, as he forced himself to his feet to pursue them – he heard them *shrieking*, and so ghastly were the noises – this, to a man who had recently served in battle – that he fell down in a swoon. Later he dragged himself to the nearest town. He spoke to the priest and the notary. His account is on record, and anyone may see it."

So absolute now was the silence also in the dining-room that when a wick popped suddenly in one of the candles, two or three of the ladies cried out.

"But," Louis said, "what *things* are they reckoned to be, in the forest?"

Madame de Lejay spoke leadenly, her eyes cast down as if afraid even to talk of it. "Vampires."

"Oh, Louis – where do the souls go, when their bodies were the victims of vampires?"

Louis frowned at Célie, in the moonlit garden of the de Lejay house. He could smell roses, vigne-de-miel... and Célie's perfume. He wished they could discuss other matters.

Nor would he say what he had read, here and there, in his studies – that any victim of a vampire became himself a vampire, too. Why, anyway, must this be the case? Surely it must depend. Who could know?

"All good souls," he said sternly, "go to God, whatever the manner of their death. I believe that, Célie. And so must you."

His sternness seemed to console her. She liked to be guided; he had observed that on the three previous occasions they had been together.

But this was the first time they had been allowed to be alone. He looked at her, her sweet face, and saw how her eyes admired him, and thought that, as well as liking her, he might fall in love with her, too. How splendid that would be.

"Célie, we must trust in God." "And – in each other?"

To kiss her was a delight. He experienced vast joy, simply because things were turning out so beautifully.

But raising his head, the perfect moment was spoiled. For over there, against the vine-grown wall, Marcellin stood, smoking his pipe, unseen till then, but *seeing*, watching the lovers with the flat, gelid eyes of a snake.

Louis stayed in the de Lejay house four days, and spent a lot of that time with Célie. He began to desire her greatly, and was also appreciative of her talents, especially when she played the family harpsichord. The parents were affable. Everyone appeared glad. Even Marcellin, Louis was thankful to find, seemed to have become grudgingly resigned to the marriage of his sister to a tradesman's son.

On the fifth morning, the whole household was up early to bid Louis farewell. He was to catch the public coach to Paris, which left the market square at seven o'clock. To his surprise, after a tender parting from Célie, Marcellin fell into step with Louis. "I'll see you safe on the coach, my dear brother-to-be. And look, here's Jeannot to carry your bags."

Louis felt an immediate misgiving. Though the general good will might have made his perceptions cloudy, he now suspected a plot. However, to resist might well give offence to the beaming parents of his betrothed. So he accepted Marcellin's offer urbanely.

In the square, a few persons waited for the coach, and soon it clattered into sight. The brown church was striking a quarter to seven from its clock, as Jeannot, his grinning face like that of an ill-treated, ill-natured dog, threw Louis' bags – rather carelessly – to their place. Then Marcellin spoke. "Do you know, I think I'll travel a short way with you, Louis."

"That's not necessary, thank you."

"No, no. I can do with an excursion. As far as Guistanne, maybe. That's about an hour off, is it not? Then I'll hire a horse and jog back. Jeannot," he added, in a jolly tone that was patently false, "what do you say?"

Jeannot only grinned.

Louis said, "But there'll be no room on the coach."

"There, there. We can squeeze in. See how few other passengers there are. You get in, Louis, and Jeannot, you also. I'll just have a word with the driver. I never met one of his sort would pass up the chance of some francs for a drink."

Very reluctantly, and still punching his brains to find a way to deny these unwanted companions, Louis got into the coach. Jeannot hopped in at once behind him, and thumped down on the seat at his side. Presently Marcellin joined them, all smiles and charm, flirting with the two wives in the coach, speaking very respectfully to the cleric in the corner. At Louis, he showed his long white teeth in disturbing satisfaction.

Louis could only smile too, and put up with it all. At Guistanne they would get out, presumably. Yet he feared they would not. Oh then, let them go all the way to Paris, if they must. There, he could make firm excuses to slough them. Even if, as he sensed would be necessary, he would then have to 'loan' Marcellin the money for lodging, both in Paris, and on the way there, not to mention the fare for the coach *back* to Arlin.

They reached the inn at midday. Here everyone got off and dined, Marcellin too, for needless to say neither he nor Jeannot had removed themselves at Guistanne.

Over the meal, Marcellin's conversation was unctuous and gloating. Louis conceived a strong urge somehow to elude him, and his servant, while at the inn. Louis had a crazy notion of hiding somewhere, until the coach had left with them. But then, of course, he doubted they *would* leave, without him. He told himself fiercely however not to be a fool. He must put up with them. For what could these two wretches do to him, after all?

He had, in the haze of blooming love and general success, forgotten the Forest of Arlinacque.

It was about ten miles, the forest, from the inn, as Louis had previously pointed out to the innkeeper.

The coach bounded off from the inn-yard at about two in the afternoon, but then, after some seven or eight miles, it mysteriously slowed, then stopped altogether.

Consternation had the passengers craning from the windows, Marcellin with them.

The driver had got down, and came round to the door. "All will be well, mesdames, messieurs. Just a tiny adjustment is needed. We'll be off again in twenty minutes."

"Twenty! Oh," said Marcellin to Louis, "let's stretch our legs, shall we?"

The carriage was unbearably hot, parked where it had come to rest, out on the road between the fields, under a brazen, pallid sky.

Nevertheless, Louis did not want to leave the carriage. He said he would remain. But, "What nonsense! Doesn't know what's good for him, my brother Louis –" and somehow, in a couple of swift manoeuvres, Jeannot and Marcellin had urgently lifted Louis off his seat and out of the vehicle.

Once they were down on the road, Louis thrust them away. "What in God's name are you at?"

"Why, I'm concerned for you, my dear. What else?"

At that very second, the driver's mate went running round the carriage. He slammed the door shut, and leapt up on the driver's box. The driver was, it appeared, already there. Next, the long lizard-tongue flick of a whip set the horses racing away down the road, the coach rumbling behind them, only a startled face or two peering back through the windows at the three men left on the road.

"My bags –" exclaimed Louis.

"Damn your *bags*. But that coachman's a good judge – he can tell who has the class, and who has not. He did just as I told him. Meanwhile, you and I, we've other business."

Truly horrified now, Louis turned to see Marcellin had produced a smart, silver-chased duelling pistol. He aimed it at Louis' head, while Jeannot stood gobbling and spitting like a rabid dog.

"What do you want, Marcellin? Are you planning to murder me?"

"Maybe not. But since you're to wed my sister, I'd like to find out if you're worth anything, you common little lout. Worth anything, that is, apart from your dirty money. What do you say? Shall we take a walk?"

They walked, of course, along the road for about two miles, by which time they had reached the outskirts of the forest.

It was black as pitch, exactly as Louis remembered it. Some crows, that were flapping over a cornfield nearby, seemed always, even in their widest circlings, to avoid the outposts of the trees.

Marcellin halted, and so therefore did Louis, while Jeannot prowled up and down behind them.

Louis had considered trying to break away. But he had not convinced himself Marcellin, who now seemed both stupid and insane, might not take a shot at him if he did so. Such guns were notoriously unreliable – and, even not meaning to wound Louis fatally, Marcellin might still accidentally do it. Besides, there was nowhere here to escape to. The carriage, in the charge of the bribed driver, was far off. And though he had heard of villages and towns nearby, Louis did not know their location. As for the inn, it was some eight miles back along the road.

"Well, now," said Marcellin. "There it is, this vampire-haunted wood. What do you say, Louis? Shall we take a stroll in it?"

Louis, naturally, had been aware this was Marcellin's plan – been aware of it, if in some vague unrecalled way, since luncheon.

He felt, Louis, a deep, ominous reluctance to enter the forest. But he knew that if he refused, this fiend, and the fiend's degenerate servant, would drag him in among the pines, or, perhaps more likely, the two of them would give Louis a violent beating, and leave him lying on the track.

So Louis shrugged. "If we must."

"Oh, yes. We *must*. Not scared, are you, dear brother?" Louis said nothing. And Jeannot laughed in his own unmusical neigh.

They walked on up the road.

After maybe five minutes, a path appeared through the fields, which led towards the forest. It was an overgrown path, evidently infrequently used. They took it. All around, the dry yellow stalks of ripened grain stood like watching sentinels at a death-march. Then the shadow of the pines came spilling down, cool, *cold*, smelling of a strange hollowness, less verdant than empty.

The silence was all at once immediate, and implacable. It was a silence like a loud noise. Louis thought, in order to be heard above it, he must shout. But he said nothing, and when Marcellin spoke again, his voice sounded only dulled -yet it had taken on a very different tone.

"I remember old tales about this forest," said Marcellin. "Yes. A place of the Devil. Look, do you see between the trees? All the slight undergrowth there is, stays entirely undisturbed. No one comes here. No one dares... They say no animal or bird will ever enter it. If ever one strays in here, it too vanishes and is never found."

He is trying to frighten me, Louis concluded. But when he glanced at Marcellin, his enemy's face was pale, and Marcellin's eyes darted uncertainly about the dim, barely-to-be-seen avenues between the pine-trunks. They were on the very brink, staring in. Yet even now it seemed to be too late. They were already trapped in some web of sticky darkness and horror, and could not move away, only forward.

Even Jeannot looked wary at last, though he said not one word.

"Perhaps," said Marcellin. He hesitated. Louis waited, hoping Marcellin would relent, and they might still get free of the trees. But no. Marcellin frowned suddenly, and said in a harsh, low growl, "Come on then, brother Louis. Onward!" And he waved the pistol.

They stepped in among the trees, and Jeannot plodded after them.

Then all the shadows dropped together. It was like the curtain of night. Louis paused, to allow his eyes to adjust. Marcellin and Jeannot did the same, the latter cursing. But the blackness was uncanny. Even the densest forest, in early afternoon, should not change to midnight – And though Louis had waited, still he could hardly see. Less shadow, then, more a fog – a miasma – sheathed the area.

Childishly he turned and looked back, and saw daylight framed brightly, in slender ovals, between the nearest trees.

Out there, less than six metres away, lay sunburnt fields and open pasture. And yet – though the glow of day stayed visible – it did not, even faintly, reflect into the forest. Incredibly, not one single shaft of daylight pierced the gloom.

Above, boughs heavy with needles and black as ink, crossed and wove against each other. Tiny flecks of sky were to be glimpsed, but they were opaque, and remote. On the forest's floor not a fragment, not a splinter of light had fallen.

"A — strange spot," said Marcellin. Did his voice tremble? Was he acting?

"Yes, it is," said Louis.

"I think," said Marcellin, "it *would* be easy to be lost here."

"No doubt."

"But we are brave, bold fellows. And you, Louis, bravest of all, so you shall be our leader." Louis regarded Marcellin who now smiled again with utmost malice. "Courage, my valiant leader. Lead on!"

It was obvious enough what was in Marcellin's mind. Louis was to be made, still at gun-point, to move away ahead of the other two. No doubt, they would soon sidle off and leave the forest, for here, despite all misgivings, the way back to the fields was yet in view, and so it must — surely — be possible to get out there. But Louis would be forced to go deeper in, and thus might lose himself, being only a tradesman's son, an upstart, an idiot.

Yet, too, Louis had noted that Marcellin at least partly believed in the legend of the forest.

How he must hate me! In his heart he really wishes me to be slaughtered here, and so never return.

However, if by going on, he might in the end avoid Marcellin and the servant, Louis was prepared to obey.

Accordingly, he strode briskly forward, along one of the smoky avenues, not once now looking back.

He tried to measure his progress in time as well as in distance. He counted minutes in his head, one minute, then two, stalking along the corridor between the trees.

But the forest began, even so soon, to confuse him. Though he could hardly see them, the trunks of the pines, crenulated and barbarous, soared up like pillars in some macabre church. Yew trees like black bears crouched across adjacent vistas, other coniferous trees, also dark and thick-furred, struggled up between, sometimes swaying a little at some unseen unfelt current of air. The undergrowth was sparse. Here and there, a skeletal bush, a dead bramble. No birds called. And everything always the same, as if – as if in passing each column or blot of tree, Louis walked in an unnoticed circle, and so passed each one again, and then again, round and round -even though the avenue was itself in fact, unnaturally, as straight as a road.

After three minutes, Louis stopped, and pretended to ease the cuff of his right boot. He had heard no more from his vile companions. They seemed to have disappeared into the substance of the pines. He supposed – and prayed – they had now retreated.

So then, presently, he did turn, and looked back the way he had come.

All evidence of external light was gone. The smothered cracks of day which had showed between the first trees, were no longer to be seen. Only the avenue could be made out, and not very clearly, stretching along its straight pillared line. And no one was there. The evil Marcellin and the disgusting Jeannot, unable to decide between viciousness and unease, had apparently made off.

Well, it was no great thing, was it? Louis had not deviated from the path. He need only retrace his steps along the aisle, and he would come, after three or four minutes, to the forest's edge, where daylight had formerly showed – and still must. He might then linger a little, to be sure his tormentors had really gone. And after that, emerge, and go up the road again to the inn, which should not take him more than two hours. Notions that Marcellin might be lying in wait for him along the route, Louis dismissed. He was beginning to think after all he had been unwise to give in to a bully. For all Marcellin was his future wife's brother, Louis decided if any further threat was tried, he would throw off his coat and make a fight of it, pistol or no.

He was about halfway back along the avenue, and had not yet identified any glimpse of daylight through the trees ahead, when a curious sound came out of the thunderous silence of the forest.

It was a sort of prolonged whining note. At first he took it for some mechanical noise – of a bellows, or cartwheel, away across the fields. Then it seemed it must be the cry of a small animal in a snare. It went on and on, sometimes becoming louder, falling off, beginning once more.

Louis halted. The noise was unpleasant. It set his teeth on edge. He wished it would stop, for now it seemed very loud indeed –

Next moment the whining shattered into a pistol shot -and then a duet of screams. They were the most appalling thing he had ever heard, frankly indescribable, combining a kind of guttural choking with high, irresistible shrills of enormous pain and fear.

Sweat burst out all over Louis' body. His guts churned and he thought he would vomit. He wished only to run away, to bury himself deep in the ground and so hear the dreadful outcry no longer.

But then, the ice-cold thought sliced through his panic. *That is cunning Marcellin, and Jeannot too. They are copying the stories, reproducing the awful shrieks of the tales.*

They wanted to scare Louis out of his wits, and had almost done so. He shook himself. Let them howl, then, if they must. He would be patient.

The noises ended abruptly. Probably they had hurt their throats.

Louis gave them fifteen more minutes, counted out in his head, before completing his return journey along the avenue to the edge of the wood.

There was no light. It had been crushed. And what he had taken for the first trees, though he walked forward into them with the determination of the desperate, did not, now, open on to the fields. Nor were they the first trees.

Had he taken a wrong turning? It was not possible. He had not left the avenue. Unless... Had the sameness of the pines and yews deceived him? Had he somehow gone astray?

He must have done. It was the only answer.

Except for one other answer he would not consider. Which was that the trees themselves had somehow *altered*, shifting to close an open path.

I will not give in to superstition, even though I feel it. I will not be beaten by old stories and old trees, nor even by that devil Marcellin.

Soon after this, moving cautiously forward in the direction he continued to judge to be the way back to the road, Louis *found* Marcellin, and Jeannot.

It was actually quite remarkable that he did so, and had he been even a few minutes, indeed a few seconds, later, certainly he would not have done. For there was not much left of them.

Louis stood rooted to the ground – as maybe the trees were not – glaring at what lay across the track: two long heaps of rusty, greyish dust, shining a little, and so able to be seen. At the end of each of these mounds lay a pair of skeletal feet, unshod, all bone. At the other end, a face rested eyelessly, like a mask, upon a blob of darkness – all that persisted of either head or skull.

But even as Louis bent over them, his own eyes starting from his own head, as if red-hot nails drove them out, the bone feet and the masks of papery skin dissolved to ash, and in an unheard eddy of wind, blew off and away among the trees.

Between the columns of the pines, Louis ran. He dived and sprang and galloped. When he must rest, panting, he crouched low against the barren earth of the forest, among its arched, craggy roots. As soon as he was able, again he leapt forward, and on – like a hunted deer.

Yet, as even Louis understood, he was clever, no fool. And he knew all this running was of no use whatsoever.

A bleak thirst assailed him. He chewed his tongue to release moisture, not wanting even to take up a bit of the bark, or the tiny pebbles, which were occasionally lying about under the trees, to suck on. He did not weep. And only once he prayed to God. But, being no fool, he sensed even God was shut out of this forest. It was a department of Hell.

Although there had been absolutely no proper light at any time, in the end, the *unseen* illumination ebbed quite away. And then the forest was as black as if he were inside a locked chest, hung closely with thick black draperies. Outside this filthy place, worldly night must have arrived. Louis felt despair. For he guessed he would never see night, nor day, again.

Despite all that, so far, he had evaded the things – the demons or vampires, whatever they were – of the forest. But he was aware too, that perhaps, just as Marcellin had, they were playing with him. Teasing.

After the true ebony black of night soaked through the trees, Louis ceased to run. He only walked, creeping along, sometimes biting on his hand, as he had done in childhood, when afraid of the big dogs of his father's country house.

But he tried not to think of his father, or his mother, both of whom he loved, nor Célie, whom he had begun to love. He tried to beat his mind into finding a solution to all this.

He would, of course, never discover a path from the forest. That much was obvious. While whatever lurked here, toying with him, was only waiting for some self-chosen, special moment to emerge, and do to him – oh God – what had been done to Marcellin and Jeannot – and to all the rest.

Finally, exhaustion covered Louis like the night. He sat down, having no choice, his back against a tree. He was so weary and *repulsed* by everything that had happened to him, that he was almost ready to confront death. Not quite.

Sitting, he felt something inside his coat grate against his side. He put his hand on it, and drew it out. Forgotten in bewilderment – flint and tinder – the means to make light – and *fire*.

Louis sat there, holding these ingredients of civilisation in his hand. He did not think in words, but in pictures. The pictures were simple, of a dry summer forest – set alight and burning.

It was then, in the instant of revelation, that the touch came on his shoulder. *First* on his shoulder, then encircling all his body, his torso, legs, arms – his face. A soft touch, or sequence of touches, almost loving, almost amorous. He did not even flinch. He struck, with one rapid motion, the flint – and a spray of flame split the dark.

Louis saw, by the light from his tinder-box, great arms embracing him, long hands of longer fingers, stiff and glittering hair, *mouths* like those of gigantic living statues –

No eyes. They had none. Had no need of them.

It was – the trees – the trees themselves. Nothing lived in the forest. It was the forest which *lived*. They grouped around him, rank on rank, circle on circle, rootless, pressing in, spreading down their needled boughs, uncoiling their trunks like serpents. Wooden claws caressed him, hair of pine-needles scratched eagerly at his face. Faceless heads, lacking eyes, opened their mouths and breathed in his essence with adoring greed.

The forest. The forest was the vampire.

From the throat of Louis issued one long, wailing cry. But in that instant, he cast the fire away from the tinder, and like a star he saw it plunge, there among the jumble of the half-seen serpents, their thirsty needles and searching spikes.

As a new scarlet light began to bloom, like the sun fallen *upwards* from below, though the floor of the forest, Louis prized himself from that unthinkable union. And as the mouths lapped and snapped after him, he flung himself once more away.

Over boulevards lined by clutching, snatching things, that grasped at him and lost him, *lost* him, torn, milked like a goat from the pastures, *bled*, he ripped his way, tossing the flowers of fire again and again among them, until the talons of their loveless hungry love withdrew.

He saw their empire wither in the flame. He saw them consumed. Yet too, he felt himself dissolving. He ran screaming on legs made only of dust.

Even so, by the vivid light of the conflagration, Louis hurtled on, the roar of a huge forest-fire all about him, amid the limbs of demons disintegrating. A rain of sparks descended.

He tumbled out suddenly – out, sobbing and praying – and out – out – on to the hard stones of – a road. A road. While at his back, towers blazed red, and ruby fields dazzled, and purple smoke streamed into the sky, and drowned, in its rivers, the moon.

Louis lay face-down on the road, crying. Sparks went on showering over him. They scorched his hands and the back of his neck, but did not hurt. Nor were his clothes burnt, nor torn; he was amazed to see it, even through his tears and hysteria.

He thought the local villagers would soon come hurrying now, if only to try to save their crops from the wild arson of the nearest fields. But no one came. No one. They were too frightened.

The fire – the forest – was a crimson cloud that bellowed up into the sky. Where there had been silence was a symphony of rage and agony.

Louis got up in a while. He trudged away from it, along the road, his head hanging, stupefied and near to collapse. Nothing seemed real to him. Not even what he had done.

It was almost midnight when he reached the inn, or so he thought. He had journeyed slowly, and the walk had seemed to take him years. Lights still shone, however, in the inn's main room, and in several other chambers above. Louis was dully surprised none of the people here looked out to see what the other light was, blaring ten miles back along the road, where the forest went on burning.

Louis himself cast one last look in that direction. The lower sky was flushed, the stars there inflamed. Then he pushed open the inn door.

The main room contained a large drunken party of some kind. Men raised their glasses and bawled out patriotic songs. In the shadowy corners of the room, beyond the candlelight, a few other patrons were quietly sitting. Louis saw the group of soldiers he had observed on the first evening he stayed there, and then the old gentleman in his strange antique clothes, who had offered him the book of legends. This ancient man perched by the low summer fire, reading, but now he lifted his eyes and met Louis' glance. The soldiers too, Louis was aware, had turned his way. Yet the drunks at their festivity had interest it seemed in none but themselves and each other.

Now the innkeeper and two of his assistants hurried in, bearing jugs of hot brandy, fruit and sweets.

Louis attempted in vain to catch their eye. He sighed. He would have to wait.

It was then that the old man got up, and hobbled towards him.

"So you have come back, monsieur."

"It seems I have," answered Louis.

"I believed you would. Despite this, I tried to warn you. Yet, the very fact that I was able to do so, to speak to you at all, indicated, alas, that already, probably, your fate was sealed."

"I beg your pardon?" Louis saw the innkeeper approaching, and hailed him again. To his dismay, but somehow not to his astonishment, the innkeeper paid Louis no attention, simply walking straight by him and out of the door. Lamely, Louis gazed at the old man in the old-fashioned coat. "The forest burns," Louis said. "Has no one seen the purple light in the sky?"

"I have, monsieur. They have." The old man gestured graciously towards the soldiers in the corner, who in turn bowed to him. "But it has burned before, the Forest of Arlinacque. Or rather, we have thought it has. For the forest, alone of all things, can never die. Nor can it ever be left hungry."

Total stillness flowed from the night, and settled within Louis like a sort of poison.

"What are you telling me?"

"I am telling you that this is now your home. As I once did, as our friends the soldiers once did, also, and as others have done, who now exist inside this inn, you entered the forest, and the forest took you. But that is over. There is no more to fear. Those persons that the trees kill, when they are wicked, they go elsewhere, and those who are saints, they too, if to another destination. But we who are only ordinary men, we come back to this inn. And the inn is full of us, dear monsieur. Look about you, and see." Louis looked. He saw. They were everywhere, at the edges of the room, on the stairs, moving between the shadows and the candles. Old and young, wealthy and poor, male and female. They were nodding to him, smiling not unkindly, sorry for him, for the shock he experienced, now, which they too, long ago, had also felt. While in the centre of the room, brilliantly lit, the boisterous, fleshly, mortal drinkers saluted each other, and saw *no one else at all.*

In a misery that seemed, even this early, quite familiar, Louis watched, in his mind's eye, Célie slipping away from him, his parents, his youth, his future, the world itself.

"I did not, then," he whispered, "escape. I thought I had."

"You did not escape. None ever do."

"Oh God, what has become of me?"

The old man replied, in the most gentle of voices, "It is nothing so very unusual, dear monsieur. You are only dead."

Fr'eulogy

And where did this horror spring from? It just arrived, as now and then they also do. Ever since, I sometimes think of it at an otherwise pleasant moment, and have to push it firmly from my thoughts.

They could be heard clearly, as they stampeded towards the room. There was normally a terrible eagerness and precipitation, an *avalanche* quality to their evening entrance. Horror filled the air. But the element in which they entered was molten joy.

They were *hungry* for what came next.

Sometimes, at other hours during the day or night, only one of this horde might enter. And then not always to do harm. Nevertheless, those who – for want of better words – *waited*, knew that torture, defilement and death might well be imminent. The incomprehensible activities of their captors were identified as a vile flirtatiousness. But now and then even, they might reach out and *fondle* one of the helpless captives, next letting them go and leaving the room, this chamber of misery and agony. After which there would fall its only peace: an unlevenable despair.

Usually however the touch or fondling preceded the act of brutal murder.

The murderers seemed to relish the screams and the sprays of living fluid, the denuding of flesh, the ravaged husk finally flung away – or worse, left some while for the rest to contemplate.

Hell was not found in a secondary world. No, it was here.

Hell was in this room.

Do I remember how it happened? Yes, I remember.

I lived among my clan. We existed in sunlight and shade,

loving and simple in our happy lives. Then predators fell upon us and tore us from our beautiful and leafy camp. In mobile prisons we were dragged, bumped and shaken, unable to move otherwise, our cries and prayers ignored, towards some gigantic structure. And here in markets we were sold as slaves.

I do not know what became of my fellows, though many I saw borne away.

By then anyway I had lost my kin. There had been only one last elder of my clan, and this one *they* took hold of, saying this one was too old, no longer worth anything. With their appalling strength they cast my elder down. Death took that life – I saw and mourned. But, as I did not yet understand, that one soul among us was spared very much.

Presently I too, with others, was purchased.

The shame. I cannot speak of it.

Worse even than any transport already endured this final heartless rush, but at its end – the room. The room of torture and death.

We lie in a circular pit.

Its sides are slippery. Even were we able, we could not climb them. But of course we cannot move; it scarcely matters.

All of us are strangers to each other – yet, in this extremity we are comrades. If we could cheer each other we should, and at first this we tried to do.

But then came two of them. They felt us over, immodest and unkind.

After which abruptly one of them seized that one which lay by me, raised the living form – and began the frightful act of slaughter.

A knife was used – *teeth* were used.

I cannot and will not say more.

What have we done that they should hate us so?

It is beyond all sanity. It is beyond all life.

Later on, as darkness fell, many others came, and worked their will, which was similar, or more ghastly.

A day after when, stunned and weeping, desolate, we lay there still, those of us that remained, two others were placed among us. They were of a different tribe, as are many of us indeed. But these two, more dreadfully, were *kin*. Out of pity, or sadism, it is impossible to tell which – *they* had lain the kindred down side by side.

So through the day they comforted each other, these two, as best they could. And we, though we had warned them, spoke little.

None molested us until the evening.

Then *they* came in singing, with a procession of lights, and flimsy things and things which they broke with a cracking noise, while smoking stuffs that stank were placed around us, and these too they tore apart – but not yet us.

Oh, their laughter. How they laughed.

At last they left us. Had we been spared?

No. Back came two, and took hold one of each of the kindred.

Each of them must watch the other, and we must watch, as they were rent apart, their vital liquor spraying, calling out to each other, but then their screams shattering like falling stars. At last only two little inner bones were left lying.

Laughing, laughing, the wicked went away.

Night had descended. But day returned. And now again the evening is close.

Tonight more of us – how not – will meet this unthinkable fate. Torn apart – *devoured* alive – for the pleasure of fiends.

I sense I shall die next. I am not brave.

I would sell my living soul for one more hour –

James Malloy goes into the dining room. Last night the birthday party had left quite a mess, but his wife had cleared the dishes by now, the remains of napkins, crackers and candles.

James paused. He looked at the bowl, considered. *This* won't spoil his dinner. Selecting a large apple, he bit straight into it, the

juice spraying lusciously.
He didn't hear the screaming.

The God Orkrem

Rage wrote this one. Perhaps many of us feel it, here and there, or frequently, or in the dark before dawn – however irrational and pointless we may still judge it to be. But then again, what may the answer demand? And what does the Defence entail?

How long I traveled I have no knowledge. When you have lost everything on earth for which you ever cared, distance—and time—become two foreign elements. To a man bereaved of all as I was, distance and time are only words.

For me then, and also now, only one word any more can exist:

God.

The god Orkrem.

I think three seasons had fled over the lands, and by then I was far away from anything I had ever known. The leaves were falling thick and red as blood when the old woman met me on the path.

"Where you go, warrior?" she asked, flirting with her old eyes as crones do, like as if she is your mother, or your aunt.

"North," I said.

"Oh," said she. "To the mountain towns."

It was beyond the towns I was heading, but I nodded. Then she said, "Watch for lizards, warrior."

"Yes, then."

"Never be impatient," she said, "with any that would help. Watch for lizards."

"Thank you, pretty auntie," carefully I said. For even then, sometimes I would take care.

But she only scowled. Behind her face of tree bark and black pearl eyes, I glimpsed a maiden with skin like snow and a rose for a mouth.

Then she was gone, and so was I.

Winter was coming on, and I had reached again another land when I met the second woman. And she was so ancient she made the first like a girl. She had no hair and her flesh was lacquered ivory. She was formed of bone and briar.

"Well then, warrior," she said. "These mountains are high enough."

I was past all the towns by then. The clouds often descended and touched the ground. I stood now in a cloud with her, and she and I peered at each other. Her eyes were not black pearl but the heads of white vipers—also blind she must be.

"Not quite so high," I found I said.

"So you must go still higher? Only the sky is there." I offered nothing. Then she said: "But the upper air is a country too. Beware of lions as you go."

Out it came before I had rein on it. "Not lizards then. Lions."

"Oh, there are lizards," she said. "But there are lions too."

"They will be no worse than life."

"Only one thing is worse," she softly said.

This was no question, nor did I answer. But in my head a voice spoke loudly as a beaten metal shield. The god is worse.

He. Orkrem is worse.

And she nodded, the ancient woman, as if she heard. And then she said, "If you were my grandson I would lesson and warn and train you, I would. But he died."

"Men die."

"And women die too," she replied. "The earth is all to die in, not to live. Not many know. But you have learned that, warrior?"

"Yes."

"Be on your way then, son."

I was not her son, nor her grandson. But her words cut me

with the sharp blade of a terrible and unexpected tenderness. Kindness I did not want at all.

In the labyrinth of agony, no beauty must ever enter, not one single whisper of compassion. Or steel breaks like glass.

The mountains climbed like the crested backs of dragons, and I strove on. I knew very well where I must get to, if it were real.

Oh, since I was an infant I had heard them preach and sing of it.

In the stone temple I had sat with the other children, and by us our own *true* gods, our fathers and our mothers, all our kin. There we were instructed by the priests.

The world had been made for us by gods, of whom Orkrem was the greatest and the most inventive. He it was who had formed the clay of the earth, and dressed it with cunning pits and traps and varied dangers. He it was too who had fashioned humankind out of some supernal wax, forming our ancestors with slow, spiteful pinches of his fingers that had viciously hurt them. So that, ever after, we knew pain first and best, and our own babies were borne in pain, screaming and weeping even before they had the water for tears in them.

Orkrem was a harsh god.

Not a single priest said why—or knew not why to say. But the earth was to be our school of being harmed. We were to suffer here, and endure suffering. Other lesser gods, it was well known, had tried to make the earth beautiful, adorning it with charming and reassuring things—the loveliness of forests and seas, dawn and sunset, moon and stars, music of birdsong, flowers, honey and wine, and even the best gift of all, which was love. Animals too they had assembled in the world. But Orkrem, when he saw that, decreed animals must then feed on each other, and humankind must feed on the animals. To ensure the needfulness of that, Orkrem next adapted us so that we should have a physical necessity to devour meat, without which mostly we would not be healthy. Therefore even the animals came to harm and pain, and usually through us. Meanwhile Orkrem made certain otherwise we might not often, on any account, enjoy the beauties of the earth. He sent us diseases and anguishes; he sent us suspicion and jealousy and dread and murder. Even love he soured, turning it like cream, so it should fret us, and drive us mad in loss or denial. Suffer we must, and endure we must, and in the end die we must, most often in extremes of horror and agony. For pain was what we entered the earth to know, in all its forms, of body, mind and soul. Pain and despair.

And all the while, from screaming weeping birth to weeping shrieking death, we must praise, worship and bless Orkrem, who was easily offended. So that any slight wrong-doing we committed, even as a reaction to his evil woundings, or in desperation, having no other recourse once his will was enacted on us, we should after death be punished for.

With such awareness I grew up. As all have grown who live upon this earth.

Though, when young, incredulously, I *doubted* it. I have no notion as to why, the proofs were already before me. But I was in my spring. My blood-red fall, my winter, still to come.

So Orkrem, the Great Artist, set on to show me the veracity of priestly teachings.

At seven years of age I saw my sister, along with others, perish of a scabrous plague. At ten I watched my mother die in childbirth, and the baby within her. At twelve an enemy came and destroyed our village. I witnessed my father's death. I and one brother were dragged away as slaves. In another place we were brutally versed in the arts of battle. We, like fools, and having no choice, allowed this, and came to shine. For these our conquering enemies then we grew up to fight as their champions, and helped win for them great renown. Freed at last due to our value, we achieved riches. We lived friendly among them, making ourselves forget they had slain our kin and were our foes. One day, I saw a young woman in the fields, gathering the sky-blue flowers for garlands. When she turned and gazed at me our hearts began to beat with the same tempo. It was the gift of the other god, who had brought love into the world, and at that time I so credited his power. Her skin was like *snow* and her mouth a rose, but her eyes were like the blue cornflowers. For her heart, Orkrem had made it. It was wax.

A few months after our wedding, she told me she was with child by me. And I rejoiced.

But as it happened, it was the child of my brother, since at him too had she gazed. And their hearts had also beaten as one. And this not fifty days after first I had her.

There are always those who will *see* and tell. They had seen, and soon they told. When the baby struggled out into the world it had the color of his hair, not mine. I let it live, as it screamed and tearlessly wept. Nor, as she screamed and shed her tears like a waterfall, did I kill her. Him though, my brother, him I meant to kill. But at the last I could not do it. I had killed so many men in my trade of war. And I had pictured *his* death, my brother's, too well and too often. There is some other lesser god who creates this magic. His name is *weakness*.

Then I must run. I ran.

Some while after, in another place again, I worked the land, and with the horses, and going one day to a temple I confessed my crime of hateful blasphemy. For this they did not punish me. They had no need. They told me Orkrem would himself see to it, since I had cursed his name. The world was made to torture men, and they must suffer it all and always bless him. One step from this path, and he would chastise them worse, during life, and after life, forever.

Later, I went on my way from that country. For years I kept my wandering course.

One other woman I met in that time, and loved. She was unlike the other, being dark, and her eyes the color of good beer. We lived in some pleasure with each other half a year, before the scabrous plague came on in those parts. Walking back beside me from the field one night, she suddenly fell down without a prelude, and was dead by daybreak. I saw to her funeral and went away. From the moment I had met with her, I believe by then, I guessed she and I would not have long.

I suffered, and all other men suffered, and sometimes, if only briefly, I or they prospered. And as I went on through all of that, I noted how most other men, and women too, proceeded always in the same fashion. All told, you could not press a slender stick between them for the misery and injustice to which they fell prey, and which in turn they dealt. We were all of us equal. We were damned.

Finally, about my thirtieth year, I reached a temple of another sort. They took me in when, all vitality spent, I dropped like the dead at their threshold. And they were kind to me— kindness which, even at that hour, not yet had I learned was the cruelest and sharpest of life's blades to cut and disable.

Presently the priest said quietly, "For us, we believe in that one god who brought love on to the earth. Believe in him, and nothing can defeat you."

"What of death?" I asked him.

"Death least of all," he told me. So sweet his face, and inwardly clean, as if his inmost soul had been washed in purest water. But less than a year after, I saw that face transfixed by a black-bleeding arrow, and all about a robber horde besieged the sacred house. I held him as in agony—what else—he died. And his weeping forgiveness of his god, the god of love, shattered what was left of any heart inside me.

When all had fallen then, black and burned, I fought a way from the scene. And so went on with my wandering, going always north, and ever upward on the sloping land. For they had taught us in my youth that the master god, Orkrem, resides on the floor of the skies.

And Orkrem was, at that last, my only destination. If ever I had had any other goal, or could have done, seeing the ruling god *is* this world, any and all of it, the beginning and the end.

The tops of the mountains rose above the cloud, which I had not expected. The mountaintops were gray as sightless mirrors, and the skies, now winter began to stir its iron wings, far grayer.

Below, by day, those lower clouds yet nestled like forests of gray ash.

Above, by night, the stars were the razor tips of knives and swords, burnished and pointing through, every one hungrily focused on some human heart.

When last I had seen a green tree it had made me think of sickness, plague. When blue I had seen, the sky reminded me of faithless eyes.

And red was blood.

A last old woman met me on the track. And she was so old she had been wiped of anything, like as if she might have been a baby stretched like a string, and so peculiarly tall. Though her eyes were like dull yellow coins.

"None otherwhere to go, warrior," said she, "but up in the sky."

"Then that must be my road, granny," I told her. "No use to warn you then," she said. "For you were warned of lizards and lions and paid no heed."

"Nor have I seen a single lizard since. Let alone any lion."

She spat on the earth, but her spit was wholesome, and only like a drop of bright water. It was almost like a courtesy when she spat. A tenderness that had no kindness, and could be borne.

"There have been lizards aplenty," she said. "They have run under your feet, and over your body as you lay sleeping. And *through* your body they have run, as if through a long cave or a deserted house, and through your brain they have run and in and out your dreams, as if through a high room in a tower. And many lions have followed you, smearing the waste of their kill in your footsteps, and breathing their hot stinking breath into your nose and mouth when you slumbered, and *stood* on you they have, heavy as mill-stones, and torn your skin with their claws." She sighed, rustily. "But you saw and heard and felt nothing of any of it. The heavens crashed on your head and you missed it. The sea came up the hill and drowned you and you never even felt its wet. Go on then. Go up the sky."

"I shall, granny."

"I am never your grandmother. I am only the very final thing of humankind you will see before you meet your god."

Then she was gone, and so was I.

But I had learned not one thing from her, as nor had I from the other two.

No man can climb up the sky.

Yet I reached the topmost peak and stood on its flat table, staring upward.

All round, beneath, the lands fell away together, but they were like a game-board, with their colors of plague and faithlessness and blood. The world no more real for me.

In the sky the higher clouds ascended like a stairway. I stretched up my arms, and for hours on end I bellowed, till my voice was gone. I called his name: *Orkrem! Orkrem!* And then I whispered his name: Orkrem.

Night bloomed its black poison-flower and the stabs of the stars pierced out.

Then a wind woke in the core of the sky.

It came forth on me like a giant bird, a dragon. Roaring, it clutched me, and whirled me off the peak.

No longer, me, with a voice to blaspheme him, only my whisper to say now he would dash me to earth and break me. But this was not the way of it.

The sky wind thrashed me not down but upward, through the cloud and through the basement of the sky itself, and flung me headlong on the floor of a huge echoing chamber that was black as the void, yet lit as if with torches.

And when the wind was gone, and the noise of it emptied from my ears, I looked and saw I was in some colossal place like a temple of pillars, but carved out of the night itself. Far away down a long avenue, the slender moon was rising, on its side like a white boat. Swollen planets the colors of sickness and betrayal and war moved slowly through the vault.

I was in Orkrem's house. The house of the god.

He did not come in for a while. Or he may have been there anyway, unseen and unfelt. He might have hung in the tiniest drip of moonlight, like a spider in its web. Or curled about the pillars like a sort of night mist, visibly invisible to me.

But then he did come in.

He made no sound. He did not even manifest—appear, as a flame would, struck all at once on a lamp. He was not. Then he was.

I pulled myself off the floor of his house, which was a solid floor, like marble—but it was air. I stood and looked at him, in his face.

He was high as the house, wide as the house. Yet too he was only the height of a gigantic man, not that much—a span or two—taller and bigger in frame than I. But he was the lizard, and the lion. I can describe him no otherwise. I *fail* to be able to describe him. Only for that—lizard and lion—or that his face was a shout like the rumble of an earthquake. And his eyes put out the light of the razor stars.

And then my voice returned.

Did he give it me? For he spoke to me, and he asked *What do you want of me?*

And then I bellowed once more at him, bellowed as out on the mountain before the wind lifted me up.

"*Orkrem—give me my life!*"

The conflagration of his eyes flickered.

You live.

"No," I answered. I knew how to speak it. I had rehearsed my words so long. "No human thing can *live* in your world. Your world is death-alive, but *life* it never is. We are *born* into death, and *live* in death, until we die—in *death*—and if, after all these *dyings,*

125

we are with you—then still it is *death*. Death through eternity, agony and anguish, terror and despair. Orkrem—*give me my life.*"

When I grew silent I heard how the temple house rocked and rang from my uproar, and from my rage and grief, that too. No single man, even one lifted into the sky, could make such a passion and din. Instead it seemed I had brought with me the outcry of every human thing, and every beast, all the complaint of the earth that Orkrem had made for us to suffer horror in.

Time passed when I was done. But time, though still somewhat it seems I had measured it, meant nothing to me.

A moment or an hour or a night or a season went by.

And then the god was beside me, so near I might have stretched my hand and touched his lizard-lion form, or his face of earthquake and volcano.

I never touched.

But he put up one hand, or as it might be one scaled and taloned paw. He passed this once across the visage of his godhead.

And then I saw. What...*what* did I truly see?

I saw his boiling and frustrated anger and his wretched hurt, I saw his tears that dropped like blazing rains. I saw into his mouth to his tongue bitten through in agony beyond bearing.

To me then, soft as snow, he said this:

"Your life I gave you, nor therefore can I give you it again. But as you have seen, and dared to tell me, my task I have Failed at. For this then, *you* shall have my task. You shall be me. You shall be a god. *You* shall make and plan and direct and rule and correct and master the world. It is all for you to do. To change as you will, to repair as you can, to alter hate to love and misery to happiness. To make a paradise on Earth. It is with you. And now, at last, at last, I shall have peace." With this he left me. But not I him.

A vast while I balanced there on heaven's floor, between aether and earth. Enormous metamorphoses shook me, with a hideous gentleness. Yet as I took on the mantle and the sacraments of the immortal life he had cast off on me, I must consider what I had been shown.

Judging by what was evident in his wounds, and his wild prolonging sorrow, it must seem he had writhed in that way for aeons. He had not then, surely, as our teachings had it, *begun* with ill intent to us—or why mourn so, as if at the ruin, not the glory, of his work. Worse, it must seem he had been unable to put anything right, however the ruin had occurred. More likely I felt it to be, that at the start of all, he had tried to make all perfect in the world, and we perfect also, that we could be glad, and create there nothing ourselves but fine things.

Yet some happening there was—either in him, through the exhaustion of all his ceaseless care and labor, or even in us independently of him. And from that came the worm that gnawed on the honeycomb, till all was wormwood ever after. And he, god though he was, could not heal such sores.

That much I had sensed in the single instant when he uttered his ultimate word, which had been *peace*.

I have no means to grasp, even now I have not, if this were some ending trick he played on me. Or some *beginning* trick of my mind, transformed so fast from clay to supernal fire.

Nevertheless, just as my huge shout had done, that subtle ending word echoed on and on, here in the god house which is now mine, and which I have grown already great to fill.

I stand on the sky and the planets turn and the stars rip their long rents through the night. The moon will sink. The sun will rise.

I am the god.

I am the maker and master.

Before me I behold multitudinous possibilities, vista on vista, world on world. But so then, once, must he too have seen them, and tried them—maybe even to the giving of the gift of love—but he had *failed*. And then he wept and screamed and had bitten through his tongue. Until, finding me, he has taken me up, and shed on me the whole of what he could not do.

Such *power* is mine. Will I then work success here, where Orkrem never could, now I am Orkrem?

I am God.

I am Almighty.

I am afraid.

In the Country of the Blind

I often write very, very long works. And once in a while, what the excellent late Donald A. Wollheim, of DAW Books of America, used to call a 'Stocking filler'. For me, the ridiculous nature of this Lilliputian-sized Cautionary Tale – is a cipher for other matters that could fill a thousand pages.

In that country, everyone was always naked. They slept naked and woke naked, got up and went about naked. No one was at all concerned or offended, let alone especially excited by this. For the thing was, they all believed that they were clothed. That is, they believed that their nakedness *was* clothing.

And so they judged each other, you can imagine, on how nice their *clothes* were. "I love that woman/that man, a man or woman, woman or man might say, "I fell in love with her/him the moment I saw her/his wonderful garments." Or, "No, I don't like the things she/he wears." And sometimes one might say, "Now I have shed so much extra padding from my clothes, I find I can run all the way upstairs!" Or another, "These clothes are old and wearing out. What a pity. When they were new they were quite splendid."

However.

One morning, into this well organized country, there walked a man wearing *actual* clothes. He had on a shirt and jacket, trousers, shoes - and under the upper clothes he even wore underclothes.

Everyone in the naked country stared at him in horror.

Now they *were* concerned, offended - even, unfortunately, some of them, *aroused.*

"Look!" they cried, ironically covering the eyes of their children and elderly relatives, "he is – *naked.*"

For they knew *they* were clothed. And wore their garments modestly at all times - even in bed, or in the bath, when swimming, or when making love.

"You are obscene! You are a threat and a disgrace!" they screamed. And, rushing at the clothed man, they tore both him and his clothes in pieces. So they found out that, under his nakedness, his dead body *was* clothed quite properly in hair and skin, just as their bodies always were. This took away all guilt. They saw they had been inspired.

They buried him at a crossroads of their country, as a stern warning to others.

My Heart: A Stone

From nowhere too this came, hard as rock, cold as ice, singing its tears like a winter wind. That, the content. And its setting is a sort of 1900 smoky, soot-rimmed over-industrialized England. But its lead protagonist, Harco. Well, now. I freely admit a lot of my characters, through the years, have been played for me on the inner mind-screen/stage-set of imagination, by some extremely talented, charismatic and gorgeous actors, only a few of whom have I ever, even briefly, met. Vivien Leigh, for example, Derek Jacobi, Jacqueline Pearce – and so on. In the following novella, the lead was taken by a man ever unknown to me aside from watching TV and theatre: Harry H. Corbett, whose fame in the end stemmed largely from his peerless portrayal of Harold Steptoe, in the TV dramas – Steptoe and Son, by Galton and Simpson, in the previous century. Corbett was in fact a superb actor, not only in this persona – elsewhere he was and is remembered for, amongst others, Shakespearian stage roles, such as that of Henry V. Yet as Harco, acting unpaid (~and unknowing!) in My Heart: A Stone, he does retain a faint ghost-hint of a past, begun off-stage in the rag-and-bone trade, and of a father even less lovable than Steptoe Père. Unlike the likeable, sad, hilarious and self-deceiving Haro, Harco has, perhaps, a better chance at life – if, conversely, a proclivity for running into things supernatural and unkind.

My unlimited admiration and thanks then, to this actor, as to them all, for such inspiration and visual help.

> *Upon this stone my heart will break –*
> *Upon this hour my life forsake –*
> *Remake my heart, I say, remake –*
> *And on my heart this stone will break.*

1

The house was made of glass, or that was his first impression of it; tall windows like vertical oblongs of water, and a vast bulb like mottled ice to one side. Above was a dome that mirrored the descending sun. All of the glass to some extent did so. Rather than ice or water then, a building of flame. Or a house on fire that burned.

It lay below him in the shallow valley to which the sombre woods had gradually led him. Farther off down there he could make out another twist of the wide road that lashed throughout this countryside, going towards or around all the local towns, with their tang and taint of coal, iron and soot. He too was bound for one of these, eventually. There was no hurry, there seldom was, for him. He took his pickings where he could, or would. And where not, he lived off the land's larder, which provided roots and game and free water, and fodder for the old horse – even the occasional smith, wheelwright and farrier who could fix the grunting cart or the horse's wheezes. He was a good one, Jupiter, the horse. Better, Harco believed, than he himself. But it was easier in some obvious ways to be a beast than a man.

By now the sun was about an hour off set.

If he wanted to try the fire-glass house, he should probably get a move on, since plenty didn't like to open up after nightfall. Jupiter however had begun to crop the grass. He had been trotting or walking since morning. Harco dropped the reins loose and got out of the cart. He rubbed Jupiter's wide grizzled neck with a tender fist. He'd let the old boy please himself for a bit up here. There was no one about, Harco could tell. He would walk down to the house, stretch his legs. If he was lucky some maidservant might take a liking to him and guide him round to the kitchen for a slice of cake and a tankard of tea or beer. It happened. He was not a bad-looking fellow after all, not yet quite forty, his gypsyish shoulder-length hair thick and curling and sable, his large eyes a sort of malt-green, and all of him tanned and well-muscled. That was the lifting had done that. And, he supposed, the odd running away or fight. Such was life, and trade.

As he started downhill, Harco glimpsed a pair of tall brown ears that moved through the longer grass at a leisurely pace. No, hares didn't flee from him, nor did any of that kind. He had the knack from his fey wild mother. While from the Dad he had only received the rag-and-bone trade, and many hundred whippings.

A rough track scrawled over the valley, doubtless heading towards the town road, and passed by the house.

Two impressive ironwork gates stood wide open, and beyond was a kind of carriage way, but rougher even than the track outside, cloven by tree-roots and weeds and littered with stones. The house showed now through dense gatherings of trees. While the falling sun struck everything in front of Harco with rich gold, but soon these groves would be dark enough.

Harco emerged on a ruined lawn. Ahead lay a terrace with broken steps and statues along it lacking heads. There was, now he had come this close, a look of utter vacancy to the house. He had already noted not a wisp of smoke rose from any chimney. Last sunlight blazoned only the upper windows. A huge silence, which was in fact composed of small non-human sounds – an evening breeze, the ripple of leaves, passage of wings – closed here like heavy curtains. In the bulb of ice – a conservatory – he viewed a cracked urn or two, dead plants like large black spiders. The main house doors, unlike the gates, were shut.

Harco rapped. He listened attentively to the distant inner echo. Despite all contrary evidence, he sensed humanity was represented in the house... people. But more than this. Some other thing was there. It had nothing to do with commerce or gain. What was in the house was death.

Minutes went by. Light flared on the roof above, and vanished suddenly. Dusk filled the valley in a moment. Only the sky still glowed. He did not try to knock again.

A star appeared, not luminous only pale. And footsteps

moved towards him from the unseen spaces behind the doors.

Was she beautiful? He thought she was, but so thin and slight, though tall almost as himself. Her waist was narrow in the long black dress. Her wrists looked as if a sharp tap would snap them, and her high cheek-bones and slim nose, her entire face, had a white transparancy. Her eyes were large, however, a dark cold grey, the irises ringed black as the pupils. Her mouth, if pastel, was full. From the wide forehead, which had made her face into the shape of an antique shield, the heavy dark brown hair sprang back, barely restrained by pins and combs. The eyes and hair and mouth were strong – and cruel. She looked cruel – judgemental and merciless. Even her breakable wrists were merciless. Her eyes were steel, and when she grew old, which wouldn't be, Harco believed, for two or three more decades, it would be steel-grey and rasp and hiss like a serpent when she brushed it. No housemaid, this. A cameo circled in jet was at her throat. Mourning jewellery. Yes, he had been correct. Death was in the house.

"What do you want?" she said in her bleak voice.

"At your service, ma'am. I deal in unwanted items you might wish to get rid of. I pay a fair price."

"It's late," she said. Behind her, shadows massed like dark ghosts in the hall. A staircase glimmered about thirteen long strides off, but fading into evening, ceasing to exist. The windows had been veiled. On a wall a mirror was turned to face the paper – ancient superstitions.

He pretended he did not know someone had died.

"I regret, I left my horse and cart up the hill, it took me a minute to walk down here."

"It is too late," she said. Her eyes did not blink or shift from his. "We have nothing for you."

"Perhaps I might ask the gentleman?"

She laughed. It was a cold, hard, steely sound.

"The gentleman," she said, "has gone away. Far off. And the

other... gentlemen – well, they'd tell you the same. But step in," she added, startling him after all, moving back and inviting him with a mocking flutter of her hand. "You can have a look and see if there's anything you fancy."

At that moment Harco, sometimes called the Hare, felt a thing like an obdurate barrier thrown up across the entrance, less negotiable than any refusal or shut door. Go away, it said to him. Take to your heels, it said. Run fast.

Harco stepped over the threshold.

Instantly he smelled it, the odour of lilies and embalmment, and the faint whiff of corruption beneath.

Otherwise the building smelled – empty. Stone, dust, forgotten polishes, water that had dripped.

He noticed the windows were not obscured by material. They had been unevenly daubed with paint or dirt. Small wonder they had caught the sunset so violently. No one had bothered with the conservatory, the entry to which he now saw down a dim corridor to his left, gloomily glazed with the last smoke of twilight.

His eyes had adjusted. Harco's night-vision was excellent, another inheritance from his mother. If this woman wanted to befuddle him and have him blunder about in here like a drunken bear, she would be disappointed.

"Take a look around," she said. "Go into any room you wish. See what you fancy," she repeated. And then she laughed a different laugh, low and nearly coarse. "I must go back upstairs. That is where you'll find us, if you care to, myself and the gentlemen. All the gentlemen."

When she turned, despite his good sight, it was like a black fish turning in night water. He watched her float up the shallow stairs. He had seen phantoms, now and then. She was too like one, he thought, to be one.

The lower floors were empty indeed. Not a stick of furniture, not a rag of curtain or carpet remained. Not even a picture, although the raddled wall-paper had in spots brighter oblongs and squares, where such things must have hung. Even the gas fitments were denuded of their lamps. The overmantles were covered only by dust, sometimes daintily scored by the traffic of insects or mice. He went down to the kitchen even, as if he must complete a ritual. And there too was nothing. Only the vast hole of the fireplace with its vacant bread oven. On the flagged floor lay the corpse of a tiny creature, a little shrew, a little curled-up shrew, mummified.

In the hallway, curiously examining it, he found the solitary mirror had no glass in its plain frame. Turned to the wall it was already blind.

He stood briefly considering the stair to the upper floor.

He could hear nothing of them, up there. Were they all dead then, her "gentlemen" – dead as the little shrew? Not a light. Darkness suspended in an opaque web.

It would be both simple and rational to leave by the one leaf of the front door she had left standing open. Out to the clean night scent of the valley and the woods.

Harco began to climb the staircase.

This room was lighted.

On the mantelpiece three candles burned, stuck down by wax, and in addition at the four corners of the open coffin, his bier, the big whitish candles necessary to such occasions, each in an iron sconce.

The candle-colour lilies were there too, held in porcelain. From their look, and perfumed reek, Harco guessed them three or four days in their vases. They were just turning, vague brown stains infecting the perfect trumpets of their throats. Pollen lay on the bare floorboards, where the candlelight sparked a nail left hammered in.

All these windows had been painted thickly black.

The one in the coffin seemed dead some while. Embalmed and left to wait. He should have entered the earth by now.

His face was like sodden paper, his closed eyes depressed in hollows. His breast appeared sunken in under the elegant shirt, coat and waistcoat. You could just see he had been no longer young, if not yet old. There was a gold chain and a watch on the fallen chest, three gold rings on the fingers of the right hand; one of silver on the left, with a ruby in it smouldering like decaying fire.

But Harco did not rob the dead. Not even the Dad had done that.

Would they though suggest it, the four persons standing there by a lacquer tray on the floor, and on the tray a bottle with a purple-red wine, and each of them with a plain little glass full of it.

None of them stood at all near the dead man.

She was there, of course. And a well-dressed older man with a neat beard, not yet approaching the age the dead one had been, nor, naturally, his decomposition. And two other men, as well-dressed as the other live one – as the dead one also, if it came to it – in proper funeral black. Both these other two were young. The taller, Harco thought, in his late twenties. The second barely sixteen, smooth-faced and clear-eyed, not besmirched by the smoky light, the dark, the wine. The death.

"Oh," she said to Harco, "how slow you are. Did you find something after all, down there? No? I thought not. His creditors cleaned him out. But I suppose you wanted to be sure."

The older bearded man chuckled.

The much younger one stared at Harco.

The tall one said, "You can tell he's a thief. Aren't you, my man? Come on. Own up. Or are you the sin-eater come to gobble up his trespasses? No grub, I'm afraid. He'll have to go to hell wanting. And you hungry."

Harco waited. He said not a word. For all the vicious manners of the Dad, he had indirectly, directly sometimes, lessoned Harco when to hold his tongue.

It was the one with the beard who broke the silence.

"Let's be off, boys, let's go down. The transport will be along soon. We'll make the jolly town by supper-time. A bit of life, eh?"

The twenty-year-old grinned. "For sure, Velden. Hi, Orlando, stop your dreaming –" this to the boy – "let's go wait outside. This cell stinks of the old man."

"We'll see you downstairs, widow," the bearded Velden said to the woman as they passed her. "Unless you want to imagine yourself walking all the way in the dark." His emphasis was sportive, and barbed. But she spared him no attention. She drank her glass of wine instead in quick sips and so drained it.

Harco heard the three men descend the unlit stair, laughter, a missed step, curses, more merriment; then well-shod feet exiting the hall below.

When the sound of them faded she filled her glass again.

"Do you want to inspect my lord and owner's corpse, gypsy? Go on. I'm sure you've seen plenty of dead things before."

"And you also, ma'am," Harco quietly said, "if you ever ate a bit of fish or meat."

She raised her brows and smiled at him. Hers was a cruel smile too.

But it wasn't until he had walked over to the dead man in the coffin, and looked down at him, that she added: "After all he might have something to offer you. I don't mean his jewellery. It's plate and glass. But something. A curiosity. Undo his waistcoat and his shirt, and see if it's worth anything to you."

Harco the Hare paused, but he felt a pressure like a hand upon his shoulder. It was strong, and urged him to do what she said. He thought it might just as well have urged him to thrust her back against the wall, drag up her black skirts and petticoats and fornicate with her. There was an element of that sexual prompting, strangely, unpleasantly, in this other act she suggested.

He undid the corpse's waistcoat and folded it back. Only then did he see the white starched shirt beneath was stained with raw fresh blood.

Her voice. "They say they bleed, the dead, in the presence of their murderers."

The blood had leaked above the area of the heart. The shirt was old-fashioned, with laces, but they were ready undone he now saw. With his left hand he pulled the garment apart.

Certainly Harco had seen the dead. Animals he had hunted and killed cleanly. A man or two another had done for, and twice that he himself had put paid to, having no choice. Never any quite like this. For the chest cavity on that left side was carved right open, pulled undone like the shirt above. The ribs stood yellow-white and pinkishly stippled, reminding him of the ribcage of a great whale he had once been shown in an exhibition. The human meat in the cavity was stale and reddish-blue, the fresh trickle of blood in fact quite thin and watery, watered wine... Someone had hacked the cadaver; they must have struck his heart clear through – And yet – yet -

"Now you behold it, do you, tinker man. Rag-and-bone man. So what's that?" she whispered, "bones and rags of flesh. But what else?"

In spite of himself, Harco had leaned close to the corpse. The compulsion, which had laid its heavy constable's hand on his shoulder, now pushed him in more near.

Harco was staring at what, in any other, must be the riven heart. Save it was not riven at all. It was complete and unmarked. Grey and smooth as an egg in its cushion of ragged decay. He did not believe his eyes. But then he did believe them. The unscathed, scatheless heart of this evidently murdered man – was made of stone.

2

When the fire was going well, Harco sat back against the trunk of a tree. The horse, untethered, grazed peacefully at the wood's edge.

After a while a collection of small green moons

intermittently glinted at Harco between the grasses. In recent years they often came to his fire. He heard the stealthy rustling of their progress as they skilfully avoided Jupiter's hoofs.

Harco's mother had been a witch. Or so the others thought, and the Dad – he had thought that too. A violent bully, he had never raised his hand to her, though he had wanted to. She could turn into a rabbit or a hare, they said, she'd be off like silver lightning over the hill. Harco smiled to himself; fools.

But he wondered what she would have made of this, now.

He turned it in his big hand. It felt heavy, solid, rough despite its polished look.

Of course it had occurred to him that what he saw might have been some secret macabre joke of theirs, some fetish, or even nastier matter, to have cut the dead fellow open, to remove his actual organic heart – either while he lived or when he was a corpse – and replace it with this object, this stone. It was shaped just like a human heart nevertheless. Harco had seen one once, in a glass case, and a diagram with it too, showing its workings in colour, about the time he was shown the whale skeleton.

The weight of the heart was intense. All the while he held it, it grew heavier. It weighed on him. But when he put it down on the turf beside him it soon seemed to draw back his hand, always the left one, never the right.

She and he had stood there in that upstairs room for almost ten minutes, he thought – the pocket-watch in the coffin gave no clue, it had stopped – before she spoke to Harco again.

"What will you give me for that then, gypsy?"

"Nothing," he had said.

"You think it's a trick? A game? You would be wrong. His heart changed to stone. He said so himself. He said it to several, now and then – and of course to me. Lutris was his name, Lutris Usburne, and perhaps I am his wife, do you think? That vile man with the goat beard is his young Usburne uncle, Velden, and the other taller younger creature is Lutris's young brother, Chace. The horrible boy is my own kin, my – shall I say? – my unlike twin, though he evolved later than I. Orlando. A corrupt filthy little fiend."

"And you Mrs," he said, "what are you?"

"Wife won't do then. Doria is my name. And now I'll go lest I miss their carriage. They're quite capable of leaving a woman here, seventeen miles from the town. Or will you look after me, gypsy, with your great strong hands and your night hair and your river eyes and your face like a handsome frog's? No. I thought not." And she went out.

He said, "When's the burial to be, ma'am?"

"Burial – what burial? There's no money to put him in the ground. Let him rot." From the dark of the stair outside she addressed him softly now, winningly. "But take it off our hands, why not. A bargain. His stony heart."

Harco stood on in the room and heard a sound of horses and wheels presently outside and to the front of the house. Then silence came back, the wind, the leaves. The last candles crackled and began to die. A dying lily petal fell heavy as a giant tear into the box. Harco stretched out his left hand only, and quickly lifted out the heart of stone. He'd touched dead things before, as he had said most men and women do who prepare or eat flesh. And the heart came up easily, not trammelled in arteries or entrails. No blood now.

The ultimate candle had perished as he picked down the stair.

He woke to see her across the fire from him. His mother. The flames were low by then, and in their dull caramelized light she dealt her cards: the Tarot, legacy of the Egyptians, the gypsies.

Her hair was just what he remembered, a storm-cloud of grey still laced with threatening strands of black. Her eyes were like his own.

Sitting against the earthed bastion of the tree, he looked at her. And next she looked back.

Never had Harco feared or disliked women, never been

humiliated by their natural powers. This much she had taught him, his mad fey mother, the witch, the shapechanger. Even dead he didn't fear her. But she had been out of the world some years. She looked so real and actual he did think her phantom was a true one.

"How are you doing, Ma?" he asked.

She frowned and lowered her eyes again. He saw she had laid a dark card-casting on the ground, galloping Death and the miserable Tower, all of that.

"Are you saying I'm for it, Ma?"

She shook her head. She pointed one long finger at a single card: Judgement.

"So if not for me, for who?" She shrugged.

It seemed she wouldn't outright speak to him, vocalize that was. Perhaps she had no voice now.

"What shall I do, Ma? Bury it in the ground – or go back and drag *him* out and bury *him*?" Her head shaken vehemently so her storm hair swung. "Was it true? Do human hearts turn to stone?" Her look said, You know it. "Yes. Yours did maybe. That was why it stopped." Again she lowered her eyes. Her lashes, like his own, were thick and jet black.

Behind her, down the valley, the sinking moon pierced a bank of cloud. The dying rays struck back against the house as the dying sun-rays had. Once more the smothered glass flared up. White fire now, but still burning.

His mother had cast another pale dark card on the grass: the Moon.

Not hearing any voice from her, yet her words seemed to flow across the inside of his brain.

When I were a child-girl, Harco, they took a woman what murdered her husband, took her though an' he beat her day and night, and she only stuck in him the skinning knife to save her life, but she never saved it, for ol' judge he sent her to the gallows. But in them times, Harco, if'n a woman kills her husband it were called Treason, for the King rules the people and the husband is a king rules his wife and daughters. So they burned her, living.

No, never even go up and strangle the poor bitch first. They burned her alive in the marketplace in front of all'n us. She screamed two minutes 'efore the flames tore out her throat.

Harco stared at the card on the ground while he heard these words in his head. Then he saw the card was only a flat slate marked a little by weather and moss. He glanced up and his mother had vanished, and the real moon which, even though it had so determinedly set the house alight again, had not shone through her, was being consumed completely by the horizon.

The rabbits that had gathered in the late summer grasses were gone too. Probably they had run away with his Ma, who must give off a far spicier psychic scent than any living thing.

Had she meant the woman Doria had done it, then, killed Lutris Usburne, and that Doria should therefore be burned alive?

He was weary. He pushed the stone object far off from him, using only his left hand. In the morning when he roused properly, very likely the 'heart' too would have altered. Then he could leave it here. You could not make your life just through obeying those spirits you met by moonlight. No matter who they were. Some great poet had written a famous play to that effect a few centuries before. You took heed, if you had any sense.

Harco the Hare races over barren winter ground. There's a hard frost down, and the sky black-blue as ink, with skeins of red and tawny stars. Beyond some woods is a field, bare now, with the grains growing in the cellars of the earth. But Harco can smell them. He can smell the white owl also, which not seventy heartbeats before swept to spear and carry away a murine animal that had ventured there. Hard times make hard hearts. Harco knows, without words or despair, the unDivine plan of the world, and how it operates, heartlessly. He races his shadow, a beautiful spectre with streaming ears. The moon is dead for tonight.

Tomorrow it will rise in splendour.

She is at the edge of the field, sat there crying. She wears rags and too-big bulgy broken boots stuffed with mildewy bits of ruined stuff. The hare sits himself also and stares at her. She does not even throw a look at him. Her tears, her tragedy, have become her world.

Long, strong, filthy brown hair down her back.

How white her skin, even though her hands are raw and her visible neck and ankles bitten by fleas. Her eyes, though reddened, the shade of the grey-silver tears themselves. She is thirteen years of age.

Then a ghastly drunken man comes slobber-slouching into the field. He is unshaven and wears a crooked hat and a dirty coat too small for his bony body. He leans down with a sort of laugh and wrenches the girl to her feet. "Shut your mither-moorthing, Dori. It was only a slap. Come and keep me warm." And when he slews off back along the slope beyond the field, she follows. Strangely — or is it strange? — the drunkard has not seen the hare, bolt upright, glaring with gas-lamp-green eyes. But she, as she turns out of the field, glances after all backward. Tearless now, her face hard as an iron nail.

3

And the town, as he had expected, was a hell-hole.

Stacks of pillared granite and marble, pitted by chemical soot, and other mess, in the municipal areas or the better streets, with soot-powdered laurels drooping over, the trees and shrubs already souring to autumn rust, rose-heads smashed on the pavements outside. While the poorer places were boxed with sallow brick, cracked and leaning, and the alleys thick in mud and muck. A background to it all, some manufactures, whose chimneys belched black by day and, after sunfall, scarlet and orange-zinc, blotting up the stars and turning the moon into blood. Hell indeed.

He had, Harco, seen plenty like this same.

This same — *thissen* — his mother's vernacular...

Harco had been thinking of her, of course, as Jupiter alternately trotted and ambled the cart through a two day journey out of the valley and on to and along the well-paved road. This was a busy thoroughfare. Carriages passed at a sprint going either way, a few other carts, or solitary horsemen. Once a fox-hunt had burst across the road, madmen and mad-made dogs, doubtless in pursuit of a single slender gorgeous auburn killer that, if caught, they would tear apart. A vixen, perhaps.

He'd thought of her, as well; *Mrs Usburne*. Inevitably after the vision or dream of Ma, and then the running as a hare. He did dream that shape-changer fantasy quite often; odd in its way, since he had never credited even *she*, his mother, could do any such thing. In the hare-dreams Harco knew every component of a hare's being, or seemed to. The muscular engines of its body, how its speed felt to it, its curious way of looking and seeing, of smelling and scenting, and the taste of land and air and verdure and darkness. He had mounted does too, in some of those dreams, and spent the seed of the buck hare to make new hares – though never woken wet himself. He was from his human body after all when he became the hare. Yet in some fashion the were-hare retained the observation of a man. Seeing *her*, Doria, he had felt only interest. Nor had he doubts she *was* Doria, that child-woman in a field. And he watched her pitiless as she, though on waking next morning he felt deep regret for her if she had grown up like that, the hapless toy of some villain, crying under the silver frost and nowhere to take herself for any comfort, not even to God.

But Harco understood too he might only have imagined his dream-seeing of her. If she was nothing to him, yet she had truly attracted his attention, and maybe for ever, however pointlessly.

Conversely the heart was – *concrete* enough. It had as well the proper form of the physical pump found in living men, not the fallacious romantic design so often drawn. This *terrible* heart, so like the repellent buildings of the upper town: the Town Hall, the mansions of mayor and merchants. Granite and marble, equally smooth and pitted, polished and soiled. Cold, hard, dead. And lying there by his left hand. Now *in* his left hand, in his *pocket*, heavy, pulling his old coat out of shape.

On the steps of the hotel he saw her again, and by then he had been in the town four further days. She wore her black gown and a little black jacket and net gloves, and the brooch with jets, and a lady's hat, a severe little coil with ebony feathers.

The 'uncle' was there with her, the youngish man with the beard.

She was pulling back from him, but he had taken her wrist in a playful yet possessive clutch.

"Now don't you be late, Doria. Once you're off, who'll get you back? Worse than some fellow after tobacco."

"And where shall I go, Velden," she replied, "or how do I buy anything, even this tobacco you've invented for me?"

"Oh, shall I give you some money, Dori? *I* have *invented* a little, as you're always aware. What will you give *me*?"

"What I always give you, and *gave* you – what you always *take*. But I don't want your lying money. Let me go. I want to be somewhere else."

"Till five o'clock tomorrow then," he said. "*Then* we start for London, in the *invented* carriage."

"Oh," she said, "London."

"So high you've flown, Queen Bee. London means nothing to you now?"

"A city made of darkness," she said, "divided by a death-black river, the sort that runs through the underworld."

But he laughed and let her go. She walked down into the square and across it, while Velden Usburne took himself, whistling, back into the gaudy little provincial hotel.

Harco had watched all this from a side street up which he had just then walked, having left Jupiter and the cart at the farriers.

He had not really heard what they said, either, the pair on

the steps, their voices were muted and he some fifty or sixty paces off. But he could see far and read lips quite well.

Harco had not been thinking he'd meet her again, Yet there she had been. At once he beheld in her that crying girl, and the oaf with his crooked hat and skinny nasty hand – *It was only a slap… Keep me warm.*

Stupid not to decipher what was between them then. The man coerced; even when she had been wedded to the living Lutris, Velden had done so – *What I always give – gave – what you always take* – Or did she flirt like that? After the child-girl, Harco thought not. Though now she stood upright and steely and put her head back to look the current no-good villain in the face. *I can't prevent you*, had said her look, *I never could. But I won't pretend I like it. Do what you want and so will I.*

Harco found he walked after her, once he had seen Velden slope away. She too had chosen a side street, and presently there again she was. She hesitated outside a church. Harco stood back against a grimy wall. How heavy the heart was in his pocket. The seam of his pocket felt likely to give and let it drop – would it break in pieces? Or be unable to break – Poor heart turned to stone – who had done it? Had she?

Notable, how her face was so white.

She had twisted the ring of the church door and let herself in. It was a weekday morning and no worship went on.

Harco let her move inside and told himself now to go away, even along to a public house for an ale. Yet after a brief space of time he crossed the street and followed her into the church.

It was very ancient. You could smell the age, and feel it too, the air layered in thick chunks soaked in mould and incense. There was not much light, the windows slender and scorched with hot blue and red. The pillars here, unlike all else, had a look of being cased in stained whitish velvet, arms in gloves perhaps, that rested their hands and branching fingers against the high roof, where a fretted golden ball, some lamp, hung like a dull golden spider. Churches were magical, naturally. Like all such spots dedicated to a god, and therefore to God. Thick sacredness thrummed. There she was, kneeling on the floor. Her head was bowed. It seemed she did console her misery with prayer.

Unable to see her face, unable to read what her orison consisted of, he slipped lightly and undetectably on to a bench quite near her, but the far side of a pillar.

He could hear now the susurrus of words, not their content.

Above Harco's head, invisible, the ears of the hare lifted up. Their quivering filaments snared every sound, which Harco might interpret.

Over and over she said it.

"Kill me then – *kill* me then – I curse you, you bloody stinking God – *kill* me then – punish us – no murderer must live – so kill me then – strike me down here in your celebrated house - *kill kill kill* me."

From one thin window red drops spilled on her off a pane of crimson glass. That was all the wound she received.

No murderer must live.

She had done it then.

She had carved Lutris open.

And before that, changed his heart to stone with callous adulterous unspeakable habits.

Harco heard her spit, quick, like a snake. "Curse you," she said, "you weakling."

And now Harco had no idea if she meant God still, or Lutris, or any of the others. Or only herself.

She rose. How gracefully she did so, and brushed off her dress, shook out the skirt. Her eyes were blind with anger. She could never have seen Harco. She went back up the aisle and out of the door, leaving it ajar. This time he did not follow.

The second dream addressed him that night. It *spoke* to him, whispering in his ears. And then hoarse music flooded through, like a sea of tin breathing: a steam-organ such as some places of entertainment kept. The song was *Her Dark Eyes*. Harco had heard it once or twice, probably in the pub he had visited before returning that night to the farrier's rented attic for sleep. In the dream though he was a hare once more, and had stolen in from adjacent countryside, up brick lanes and cobbles, and over a bridge straddling a putrid canal. The gambling-house with the steam-organ was wedged in an alley. It had been lit with flick-ery gas and swagged with cheap drapes. Here they cast cards that had, by now, nothing – or not much – to do with fate and circumstance, and flung dice that had nothing – or very little— to do with skeletons, and death. Gin was poured in unclean goblets, medicine for the sick who wanted not to be well. But there was brandy too, and French liqueurs, and cigars.

The hare crept carefully by. Despite its squalor, the rich frequented this den.

At a table, red, black, pale, a wheel is turning. A very tall man leans forward as it spins. He has on over-elegant evening dress of black and white. His face is lax and basted with sticky sweat. Beside him a girl, about sixteen? You cannot be sure; she is so graceful yet so – *misaligned* with this room. Such white skin, the bare shoulders and arms, her neck, her face... her silver eyes stretch wide, pupils shrunk either from some sort of alcohol, or the relentless light. There are expensive combs in her brown chestnut hair.

The wheel chatters and ceases to spin.

The sweating man gives an oath.

Rounding on the girl, he awards her a small predatory shake. "You jinxed me, Dora. Don't look at the damn wheel when it goes again. Don't you want I win? Come on, Dora, have a swig of this," putting a violet medicine to her mouth. She has a sip, and smiles at him fawningly, and by now her eyes are almost white as her face.

When the wheel begins once more to rotate, she glances down instead at the hare, which shivers near her on the thread-bare plush. And then she laughs, throwing back her head, and the arch of her throat is like the springy string of a drawn bow.

As it turned out, the man Harco had heard recommended, on the long street near the municipal gardens, was away. Harco left, even so, a few items for the absent dealer to peruse. Meanwhile among the streets of the shabbier better houses, he bought the odd piece of goods, and had a swift canoodle, too, with a fat pretty maid-of-all work he had met before, elsewhere. In the worst areas he bought a couple of knick-knacks for a slight if decent sum. He did not really want them, but you never knew, and at least the sellers would get some dinner that week. He also handed over gratis a copper pan to an old woman who craved it, telling her he was glad to get rid of it.

Less than a quarter of an hour after, at a crossroads near the town market, Harco caught sight of Doria Usburne once more. By then it was nearly four o'clock. She was in the shadow of an archway, handing to the youngest man of the trio – the clear yet ill-eyed one, Orlando, her brother she had said – a note of money; its ripe sheen wasn't to be missed. "Go on then," she rapped – Harco read her speech perfectly – "I'm not coming with you. I had enough getting shot of Velden." And Orlando grinned and darted away. But she stalked through the arch, and buildings hid her. How masculine she had seemed just now, the worst sort, harsh and rigid. It was surprising, bizarre.

He had gone on thinking about her anyway, couldn't seem to stop.

Even when he was cuddling the girl in the scullery, with the pots and jams shaking on their shelves, he had some vestige of *her*, Mrs Usburne, *Doria*, Dori, Dora, winding about through the back of his mind. Rather than lessen pleasure, this had augmented it.

As much as any fascination with her, though there was plenty of that, there was the mystery; the body left "to rot", the men – older, younger, young, the barbed edges of all they said – to him, to each other. And the heart. It went without saying, the heart.

Harco had known weird occurrences often, tiny miracles, curses, poisoned haunted spots – in houses, woods, in men.

But this. And *she*. And it.

Never ever anything of this sort.

Tomorrow he would be taking the city road. It had always been his plan, not triggered by hearing Velden's reference to London. If they meant to leave by five o'clock today, by the morning they would be far ahead of Harco.

Let them go. They hadn't escaped him. The spirit of them all was still with him, here. And, in some unease-provoking manner, his with them, apparently.

Because of all that no doubt, and of his second sighting of her, he was not overly amazed to see her a third time that evening. It seemed in fact essential that he *must* see her, somewhere or other.

Dusk was starting, and one of the better houses had been lit inside and out with a lot of lamps and flambeaux, and herds of carriages drew up outside. She stood on the opposite pavement, and next to her was one of the men, the tall young one, Chace. He wore evening dress, and she too – black still, with jet pins skewering up her wayward hair. Over all the noises of coming and going Harco heard what she said: "I don't wish to be here, and well you know it." "Stuff," said Chace arrogantly, "of course you do, you harlot." And with that he steered her almost violently across the street, and they were lost in the crowd milling forward into the house.

It seemed to Harco he was being shown continuously, asleep and waking, symbols, *emblems* of her existence.

But what about the coach to London – they would have missed it. Or had he mistaken them? Had that not been Doria, or Chace?

At the farrier's Jupiter had been reshod and burnished and given a luxurious repast. Long ago Harco, his mother's son, had taught the horse, then not two years of age, how to lie down if he wished, to sleep, resting all his body, and equalizing the flow of his blood, as a man would.

"You're a handsome fellow, Jupiter," Harco told him, "Well worthy of your name." But Jupiter dubiously nosed the dragging pocket, with the stone in it.

The farrier had never mentioned the pocket. And when, after a jar or two of ale, Harco dined with the farrier, his nice round wife and two sturdy sons, they only spoke of business generally, told jokes and laughed, and later chorused beside the black piano that Mrs played so cleverly, and which Harco found for her last year. None of the songs was *Her Dark Eyes*. That was an old song, current Harco thought during the wars with the French, about ninety years back, though it was still sung here and there.

When he got up in the loft, Harco sat for a while. He marvelled at the happiness of families such as the farrier's.

It wasn't that he was afraid to sleep only that, well aware something would be waiting for him again, in there, down inside the secret other existence of the surreality, Harco delayed, preparing himself, allowing also the *other* to prepare.

He blew out the candle around midnight, although tomorrow he would be about by six. He lay back and pictured Jupiter calmly sleeping on one side. And then the underworld drew him quietly down.

4

She slips out of the shadows. Just now shadows are all there is, an interweave of them. They might represent trees or columns, broken walls or high cliffs. You cannot be certain.

"Go careful, Son," she says, Maritara, his ma.

He nods, and she's gone. And then the shadows are becoming a type of avenue, though of what who knows.

He walks along the avenue since that is plainly where he

must go.

Partly Harco anticipates the house in the valley will materialize out of the gloom, but instead he comes on a kind of long, low shed. There is smudgy light on the general darkness, and the sound of faint lapping, as of tired-out tidal rivers. A sick-sweet bitterness drifts from the shack. Harco knows the smell. It derives from opium.

He steps back, and exactly then two young men emerge giggling and staggering from the shack, bent nearly double to avoid the ground-sagging doorway.

Contrast to all, they are well-dressed. They would too somehow resemble each other, if it were not one is so slender, and the other obese. His is an obscene obesity that has entirely wiped away all character not only from the body but the face, which is now a balloon mostly swallowing tiny lips and nose. But the eyes... Harco sees them glitter. Squeezed almost out of identification, they are like two pin-heads. Only by their glitter can you see them – that, and this other thing, at first obscure, though Harco's skin *crawls* at it. This other factor also imbues the obesity, making it not slovenly or ill-fortuned, let alone voluptuous, but *revolting*. *Vile*. For its cause, and the cause of the glittering miniscule eyes, is the *same* cause. An insatiable hungry evil. It wants and intends to eat. Set before it a hundred vast meals fit for giants – it will devour them all, and then come smarming and destroying after anything else it can get. It would eat the Earth if it could, and still be greedily starving. It would eat a galaxy, a universe. *Never satisfied.*

From the eyes alone Harco knows who this is, even if in all other respects the stranger does not resemble him. As Velden scarcely resembled the drunk fellow in the field, or Chace the gambler – and any way, Harco has been shown them this time in a different order... as if to muddle him?

Guts here is Orlando. Her brother.

She, undeniably, is the other young 'man'. She wears a man's smart day clothes, garments so narrow against her companion's bursting garb it is farcical.

Her hair has been cut virtually to her scalp. Like that of a convict.

They lean on each other, still amused.

He says, "I saw huge palaces made of angelica and cream sailing to the sea."

She says, "I saw *you* in a bloody coffin."

Orlando seems not to mind that. He chitters louder. Then checks.

"By God, see there, Doralie, is that a rabbit on that barrel? Look. Sits there staring, with its ears right up like horns."

She does not look. She pushes at Orlando, who would need a six-horse team to shift him. "Who cares? Let's have some wine, and supper. A girl or two."

"*You?*" he says, all slimy contempt, "a *girl?* You're such a woman, Velden says that of you. And Chace. Such a woman. You wouldn't dare."

"Watch me. You'll see."

"Oh, I'll watch, girlie – *girlie* with a girl."

And they swing off along the tow-path or whatever it is, disappearing round a clump of shadows that may represent other shacks. But the oil-lantern light is fading. There's just the fleeting image of a creased Chinaman with mournful eyes, who glances out from the hut, then slams its door.

Harco expects to wake now. But no. His mother once more passes and points up the path before vanishing. So Harco walks on, and through a gate of wrought iron.

Is this the pre-ruinous park of the valley house, or only the municipal gardens in the town?

There is a sort of grotto with trees, and a plinth with the copy of a Greek statue on it, this one equipped with its head.

No opium smell here, not even of town air flavoured with furnaces. The atmosphere is clean, yet empty. And silence hangs like washing from the vague trees. Not an urban street-lamp, not a star or moon. Yet just enough light presides, and reveals a man sitting on the steps of the plinth.

He looks himself, this one, enough like stone to match the statue. His skin, clothes, hair...

"Good evening," says the seated man of stone courteously.

Harco's frozen. Regardless of Orlando's comment, he is human in this part of his dream. And he feels – not fear, but terror, that eldritch classical state only visited on men by the genuinely supernatural. He has felt it before. He knows what he cannot do – move or speak. He simply waits. For he is finally in the conscious if unalive presence of the instigator of all this: Lutris Usburne. Last witnessed lying dead, and beginning to decay, in the valley house of sun-moon burning glass.

Notwithstanding everything else, it is as if they have spoken before, had quite a few meetings. The stony man seems familiar to Harco, even the inflexions of his educated voice. It is as if, Harco surmises, Lutris belongs to Harco's own savage family. He is some relative – never met, but bearing unmistakable evidence of familial traits – an hereditary nose, for example, or constant mannerism. Though it is not that, obviously.

"Have you fathomed it yet?" Lutris inquires.

Harco can't speak. Which scarcely matters, he has nothing to say. Or reckons he has not.

Lutris sighs. His grey face shows the humour people may when worn out, or deeply depressed. A sense of the funniness that others can still leap and bound, even if one day, very likely, they will not.

He remarks: "But you have the psychic ability, surely? From... Ah, yes, your mother. Not so strong in you, although it may grow. Exercise the psychic muscle, dear sir. Make it work."

Harco's tongue loosens. "What is it you're wanting, Mr Usburne? *Do you want your heart returned?*"

Lutris throws back his head, as some do, and laughs the couth hilarity of utter despair.

155

"No, no. You miss the point entirely, my dear good gentleman of the rag-and-bone business. That weight in your pocket – for sure it was mine. It was what my living, beating, urgent heart became. But my difficulty, kind friend, derives not from that. Listen now. What wrecked me was this: I was corrupted once, then twice. And by then I had been so stained and spoiled, I went on with the work and corrupted my own self. Pay attention now, if you would. This is what's important." And with that command, Harco finds he is the Hare. He sits bolt upright, and his ears stand high not to miss a word.

"I was," says Lutris, "the son of a rich enough man, who made his money with reasonable honesty, that being all we may hope for in most cases. My father died when I was some nineteen years of age. And thereafter my Uncle Velden came to share the family fortune. By one of those quirks of timing, he was a little younger than I, but he was more knowing in the ways of the world and its filth, and he put his little mind and his great and jealous spite into the service of depraving me. I had been quite an innocent, but he did very well in altering me. And after him, my younger brother, Chace, having learned such pastimes already, undertook to wean me to other vices; gambling, gluttony, drunkenness. Even when I had sloughed these two foul geniuses, their Influence remained to shepherd me. More, it remained *within* me. I fell into sink after sink of an unending abyss, till in the end I was a ravening *imbecile*, an addict of all and any crime of indulgence, *myself* a minor demon – taught by the master-devils, Velden and Chace. I could not stray, by then, from the path they had put me on, that snaking primrose path the colour of envy and venom and liverishness, and strewn with those temptations no sane man would halt to look on. My heart was sliced in two pieces by then. One side tried persistently and bravely to pull me from the abyss. But the strong, rampant second half *dragged* me ever deeper. Until, inevitably and unavoidably, all this killed me. Oh, I deserved my death. But not the limbo that now retains and imprisons me. For I'm *stuck*, my good friend, between all possibilities. I have been split, dislocated from my *self*, denied my necessary punishment which – perhaps, at last – may scour corruption from me and set me free. Thus, Harco, can you mend me?"

Harco stares with his luminous hare's eyes in the dark garden of that otherwhere.

Human words rise, ludicrously, from his thoughts, and sound aloud.

"And your Mrs – your brown-haired wife? What was her part in this?"

The stone man shouts. "I had no wife, *you simpleton!*" He springs from the steps. "Oh God – have you missed it *all?* There's no hope then – I'm lost."

At which, in a shock like white lightning, Harco woke, a man rolling from his mattress with a cry. In the morning, the farrier's wife would chide him, and he apologize – "A bad dream," he would say. Lutris Usburne had had no wife. And she, Doria, and the other three – they were long gone up the London road in some carriage that certainly left later than five o'clock the previous day. Or Harco had dreamed *everything*.

5

The road poured from the sooty suburbs and away into a countryside at first tarnished, in due course rain-washed, light-painted and immaculate. Villages lay sometimes along the road's edges, or were seen in the distance over fields, on hills. Or a fine house might tower up with grounds and woods. Once two deer crossed the road, not glancing at the man, his horse and cart; Jupiter was not trotting, only ambling. Occasional faster traffic did go by in either direction, never at that stage a great deal of it. When the evening sun began to leak red honey, Harco led Jupiter off the road into the trees, to a quiet place with a small shadowy pool. There was no hurry, Harco believed. He'd *missed* it *all*, presumably including any racing metropolis-bound coach. There was therefore nothing more to do, to say, or to think.

Nevertheless, he was aware he would dream of the Usburnes, of one or some or all of them. Of her. Decidedly, of her.

Harco the Hare runs through young night forest and its shattered diamanté of fireflies, stars, random inexplicable dew. He has an aim, the hare.

The hare knows this, but not what it is, or why. Or how.

Stone. Something stony hangs heavy even on the flying hare, whose own heart is like a ready flame. But you can strike a flame from stone. Or with a stone crush out a flame.

For a long while the hare has been running, and senses that also. Then he comes out from the trees at the edge of a wide road. The hare pauses.

No moon lights up the vista, but for the hare the stars give light enough.

The world changes.

Down the road rushes a compendium of colossal noise and splashing glare, which arrives so fast it seems like an incendiary whirlwind or tidal wave. A kind of cloud foams up and back from it like spray, and as it speeds nearer its voice is a storm of pounding and grinding, growling and rattling. Nightmare shadows are flung behind it. They burst on the tree trunks like battle shells of bright yellow and swarming black. The hare, upright, petrifies.

Nearer and clearer, more near, more clear –

Other shapes tear before the tempest, ahead yet integral, ground-striking flash of iron and uplit whips of hair.

Far back in the hare's brain the man manifests. Harco knows, dimly and without conscious reason, the charging apparition is only a carriage and four, the horses going flat out. And lanterns with burning oil cause the effect of bursting shells. If he could, Harco would convey to the hare he has become that they need only stay put and let the infernal contraption pass. After this the night will be still and cool again.

But he can't inform the mind of the hare. Who suddenly, from total stasis, flares to life and dashes in the one direction he must not – straight into the roadway, between the pelting hoofs.

The horses all let out a sort of whinnying scream. All four jerk sideways – together – apart – galvanized to crazy fright by the spurting ball of darkness that has sprung at them out of the ground.

A piece of wood and metal gives with a sharp *crack*. Poorly-made shafts are snapping at violent awkward stress. The horses plunge, oddly coherent, and all at once have broken free, their wood and leather accoutrements spraying off as if mashed by an invisible force, and showers of flame-gilded splinters go swirling. A single hoof catches the hare. The hare is whirled off too across the night, lighted then darkened, swallowed up. Miraculously relieved of every shackle, neighing and shrieking, the horses plunge as one away. The coach is left to spin on the spot. Where is the driver? Gone too, gone – A big wheel evades its armature and bowls playfully along the verge. Lanterns explode. Becoming audible now, the orchestra of human screaming, disintegrating glass. The vehicle topples on its side and skids like a demented box over the paving, while showers of molten sparks erupt from everywhere, fireworks to put out the dark.

And then the gigantic tree, as if prearranged, bounds out to meet the carriage. This must be the largest of the trees in the forest, the father of the forest – World-Tree. The collision.

It is deafening. Blinding. The whole night goes up in gold and blood and thunder, and a carmine rain of bits like burning eyes is cascading through liquid air.

Deep in wayside grass the hare lay watching. Fire spangled his optics. He was unhurt, for under all he knew he was a were-thing, not flesh and bone and muscle and fur, not at all. Harco, through hare-sight, watched too. The outcry and agony had ended inside the blazing carriage. Harco did not think about this as a man would, nor as a hare. But he went on watching through an eternity, until the night and the fire were drained, and then peacefully woke as a man, in the bivouac off the road. Jupiter was mildly grazing, and the birds circling the dawn. The only smell of smoke rose from the dead campfire.

It was some three days later, in the middle of the afternoon, that he saw the wreck of a coach lying among the trees at the road's edge.

The assemblage had collapsed in charcoal formlessness. The recent rain had smudged it all. Harco noted that neither the big tree, nor any plant, carried a mark of the accident beyond such smudging.

He guided Jupiter to the verge and then jumped down. Surely others must have done this, gone to look, the criminal, the concerned, the simply curious. The road was busy enough, if deserted for a second now. And initially the catastrophe, whenever it had happened – for the timing of it all seemed strange and out of kilter – would have been spectacular. Had any of them survived? Harco had wondered this often since the dream, about as often, really, as he had again told himself a *dream* was all it was. Had the driver been flung clear – gone for help? And the maddened horses, where had they ended up and who had found them? And she. What had happened to her? Trapped in the coach of course she would have died, burned like a witch, or that murderess Ma had spoken of, the one who committed Treason against her husband. Had the ones in the carriage been able to scream for two minutes as well, like Ma's woman, before... Before.

Grim and silent, Harco stood and stared between the trees at the shards and little mounds of clinker. Were there bones? Was there the dust of hair?

"So it's you, gypsy, is it, at last?"

She spoke behind him. Harco did not move.

She said, "Oh turn round and look at me. How slow you are," she added in her cold, sad, spiteful, musical voice, and just as she had said it earlier. "I suppose you wanted to be sure."

"How'd you escape it, ma'am?" he asked carefully.

"I didn't *escape*, you fool," she grated, and then he heard the stony tones of dead Lutris in her voice. "Turn and look at me. You won't be changed to salt, I doubt you will."

So Harco turned. And he looked.

She was as he recalled, pale and slender in her mourning, and her hair still strong and her eyes like mercury in a glass. "Are you ghosts?" he asked. "Is the carriage a ghost?"

She smiled and looked away. She said, "You know it, and *you* don't. So I must tell you. Though you managed quite well so far, you and that rabbit you become after sundown."

Over with the cart just off the road, the horse stood very still. And now and then a vehicle or rider went along the road, not sending even a glance their way. Harco had brought the stone heart with him, of course he had, he had had to, there in his pocket. He took the heart up in his left hand, moulding it, listening to her. It weighed very little now, he thought.

"Lutris Usburne named me *Doria*," she said, gazing miles off, "after a land of brave people from some myth or other ancient tale. I have no true conception of this, only that he did so. Orlando, my *brother*, Lutris named after some character in a famous play, by some poet I forget. Lutris thought this boy a weakling and a chancer, though he was the play's hero. And our Orlando, evidently, was far worse than any of that. Velden, Lutris's uncle, and Chace, Lutris's brother, already had their own real names from their baptism. Both those dissolute wretches died years before Lutris's demise. But as Lutris told you, bone-and-rag man, they left their corrupting wickedness alive within him, a pair of spectral personalities that would govern and coerce his own. Ghosts, then, if you want – of a *sort*. And what was Orlando? The worser part of Lutris's own self – which in the end claimed him. Orlando, my brother. The murky half of a thing that was, in Lutris, cloven in two, one part evil, and one... good. A *better* half – what a man's wife may be called. To Lutris, therefore, it was female, lacking all male strength and authority, yet forever urging and straining to pull him from the thousand foetid brinks he sought. His male demons he saw in generally distorted forms. But she – he saw her as a girl child starved and abused, a young woman detained in dens of drunken villainy, and sometimes also depraved herself, dressed up as a male, apeing mankind's most notorious ways." Her eyes had refocussed and changed to steel again. "So, Harco the Hare. Who am I?"

In the left hand of Harco he felt sharp heat inside the stone, and how it jumped abruptly, as if living, one single beat.

"You are his heart," he said. "The real one."

"I am his heart," she answered. "And *they*, those three *gentlemen*, obliterated by dream-engendered fire, were his other natures, that lived in his heart – in me."

In Harco's hand – the softest, most subtle detonation. Opening his fingers, he saw his large palm heaped with greyish crumblings and powders – all that remained of the dissolving stone.

"We were ejected from Lutris's corpse," she said, without emphasis. "That was what carved him wide. Not a knife stabbing in but his torrent of sins and rages and sorrows tearing out. Yet while any of us, we four, persist, my gypsy, Lutris stays jailed in Limbo. Well then. *They* are gone." She raised her chin and looked into his face with a force he had never beheld before in the eyes of anyone, female or male, quick or dead. "But *you*," she said. "Only you," she said. "The *stone* heart is broken. Here I am. You must do it now."

Harco shut his eyes then. And then he opened them. He let the dregs of stone trickle from his grip, and lifting his great left fist he struck her with all his might, catching her white throat just below the jaw. He heard the bones of her neck instantly give way, a fearful noise, like no other, even if he had heard it twice before. And she fell straight down to lie in the grasses, among the remains of the carriage. He knew neither she – nor it – would lie there long. Like the heart they would crumble into dust, and feather away. But he'd not linger to observe.

Weeping he went out of the wood, and laid his head on Jupiter's kind and patient side a moment or two, perhaps a whole minute. After which Harco got back into the cart and gently flicked the reins. And up the road they went, on through the dull sun and the late summer weather, and all the seen and unseen tumult of the Earth.

Killing Her

Somewhere or other I noticed a competition, the stories for which must be encapsulated in a very small amount of words. I had no intention of entering. But I couldn't resist the challenge of coining something to fit inside that so-tight glove. However, jealousy and murder can get in almost anywhere…

Have you ever wanted to kill anyone? Probably you have. *Most* of us have, I suppose, sometime, somewhere… someone. But it passes. It goes off the boil, like a turned off kettle, or an egg. Or the passion of love. Although, if it really *doesn't*, then perhaps you have to do something about it. Don't you.

I had hated Tooty Wilson from the day she arrived. The name alone set my teeth on edge – Tooty. What the hell did that come from? Of course, someone asked her. "Oh," she squeaked coyly, "everyone calls me that. Since I was at college." Which was, presumably, only a few years earlier. I never, I think no one ever, learned her *real* name. Even emails and letters that came into the workplace for her sailed under the flag of 'Tooty' – or failing that, once or twice, *Ms T Wilson*.

She was young, about twenty-five most likely, though she looked, dressed and acted like a very well-off sixteen-year-old. Even to baring her fat little belly in cold spring, through variable English summer, to frigid, leaf-leaking autumn. Her navel was pierced as well. One gold ring. She was a plump girl, and lots of us can get easily overweight – through unavoidable medications, low metabolic rate – but Tooty, as you could see pretty fast, built up her solid curves via expensive junk food. I'd quite often noted her, still conscientiously at her desk but keyboard shoved aside, eating a double burger and fat-glittering fries with five sauces, a large chunk of cream gateau to follow. She was also, between meals, inclined to sing while she worked, which she didn't do well. Her renditions of *Cold Play* and *Snow Patrol* didn't flatter the originals. I got tired too of inadvertently typing love-and-despair lyrics into my own reports. Her voice was not only bad but infallibly intrusive, and as luck had it hers was the next position to mine.

However none of that, surely, is enough to furnish the full-cry antipathy I felt for her. Admittedly I disliked her smell, her chemically-nuanced scent, of which she always used a lot; it seemed to have given me, by the end of any day when both of us were mostly at our desks, a sore throat. Also she was prone to take – that was, steal – unnecessarily, you could always get supplies – papers, clips, pens, and other useful objects from my drawer. Once I came back from a meeting and found her using all my colour pens to mark out some sort of colour-coded gift-shopping list, on the back of a memo I had carefully printed up an hour before. She routinely stole biscuits from my tin.

"Oh," she'd say, "didn't know you wanted that." Or, "But you've got one left."

What was left that I wanted, by then, actually was simply to slap her. But I was only just starting to boil, just a bubble or two of blind allergic loathing dancing on my surface. She had only been with us all for six months. And she seemed so satisfiedly *innocent* in her carefree, infuriating ineptitude, everybody else appeared to have bought in and not to be aggravated. Sometimes they were even amused. Or worse, protective of the awful girl.

"Come on," said Rod to me, as we stood at the coffee machine, "she's all right."

"No she isn't," I said. "I don't like someone leaving smears of Tiramisu on my mouse mat."

"She's just a bit – well. She's really okay," smiled Rod.

Everyone liked her. The guys fancied her, maybe. Our one gay woman maybe did too. The other women, all in their thirties or forties, seemed to feel strongly motherly.

I considered, while lurching or crouching in the tube on the way home each night, whether perhaps Tooty *was* perfectly *likeable*, but she had done me some filthy injury in a previous life, for which Kama remained unpaid.

It was twenty-one days after she started to sleep with Rod that I decided I was going to kill her.

I'd better explain, there had never been anything, except an office friendship between us, Rod and me. We used to talk over coffee, sometimes have lunch together, or go for a quick glass of wine after work. It never went any further. I might not have minded if it had, but I'm not sure. I'm a lonely sort of person, where I can be, a *loner*. I like my privacy, and things done the way I want. Of course I had found with other people, definitely with men, that doesn't make for a lasting relationship. Rod anyway was six or seven years younger than me. And I'd never been fazed, I have to say, by the string of girlfriends he had in his private life. I'd met a couple, average, slim young women, with dark hair. Tooty was blonde, and fat. But she and Rod suddenly began to be an item. I found that out when I came out of the lavatories, and spotted them necking like kids in the corridor. They didn't spring apart, but just sort of leered at me, and she giggled. In the most peculiar way I read triumph in that giggle. No doubt I imagined this. After all, why would she *care*? And even he never seemed embarrassed. They went back to their kissfest and I back to my desk. Rod and I just didn't have lunch or coffee or a drink together ever again.

But soon the dreams started. They were all different, and all exactly the same, and in each one I killed Tooty Wilson.

I pushed her under trains, both tube and overland. I thrust her out of a plane about to touch down at Dublin, while a dream steward stood by amazed. I shot her in the chest, back or head – with a bow and arrow seen in an old Sean Connery Robin Hood movie, a twelve bore hunting rifle and a 1940's Mauser from some other filmic violence. I stabbed her with broken window glass and a fruit knife from Debenhams. I poisoned her with chocolates, venom injected with Christiesque aplomb. On each occasion I watched her death-throes. And although asleep, I loved every minute.

Never in my life before – or so far after – have I ever felt such an overpowering longing to murder another human being. But by the time I'd experienced approximately thirteen such dreams, I knew I had to act the murder out. At my hands Tooty must die.

I baked the cakes on Thursday night. I'm quite a good cook, and sometimes I do bake; it makes a change from reading. These ones though weren't my usual plain type, but full of nuts and jams, and thatched thick with frosted chocolate. I didn't eat more than a mouthful, most went out for the birds. Two I took into work, and these, obviously, were a bit different from the others.

At the afternoon break I removed both cakes from their wrapper and put them where Tooty could see. Rod and several others were in Edinburgh till next Monday, so there was no chance either of Tooty diving off to linger at the coffee machine with him, or trying to share with him any spoils.

I pretended I remembered something undone, got up and went briskly out.

When I came back one of the cakes was gone, and there Tooty sat, still chewing as she stickily tapped at her console. She glanced my way: "Don't mind, do you? Couldn't resist. Promise I'll buy you a cake tomorrow." I shrugged. She'd never replaced any pens or biscuits. I put the other cake back in the wrapper and dropped it in my bag. I'd destroy that one later, it wasn't fit for birds.

Dreamily through the rest of the afternoon I sat at work, acutely blissfully aware of Tooty, tapping and wriggling and singing and slowly *dying* not two metres from me. Every revolting habit of hers had become an exquisite pleasure. Her occasionally loud breathing, the awful soprano, her grunts and squeaks, the fat creak of her firm bulging thighs on the plastic chair, the twinkle of her nose-stud. Never had an executioner so enjoyed her client's last meal.

By the time six-thirty came, I rose in a sort of drunken trance, and turning back to Tooty from the doorway, for probably the first time since her advent, I smiled at her. "Night, Tooty," I said. *Night-night.*

Friday I took off. I pleaded an emergency dental appointment and agreed to give up instead a spare day I had owing.

It was a happy and relaxed holiday. I went shopping and bought new boots, and had some wine with lunch, and saw a movie, and went home practically a new woman – or rather, my old self.

The weekend was fun too. I did a few things I hadn't for months, including a visit to the museum and a long walk through Regent's Park. Every time something reminded me, which was often, I would draw in a sweet deep relaxing breath and think: *Tooty is dead.* A couple of times I laughed aloud, and got the expected funny looks. Who cared.

On Monday the office was back to its usual crowded self. Rod was full of the Edinburgh deal, and even came over to tell Tooty all about it in graphic detail. I started softly laughing again seeing the way he went on talking to her, so animated and proudly full of his own cleverness, when all the while the fat young woman who sat there goggling at him, in just the way she would eye a chocolate cake, was in fact quite dead. And when the two of them went out to the coffee machine I just had to go out too, simply to walk past them and marvel at how he stood there, squeezing the pudgy shoulders of a corpse, and greedily kissing it on the mouth.

Naturally, everyone treated Tooty as if she were still healthily alive. I suppose even I did, in a sort of way. But I *knew* I had killed her, that was the point. I had filled those two cakes with poison, and she had eaten one of them, and she was stone cold dead. Or, for me at least, she was.

What had I put in each cake? Perhaps you'd like to know. Half a carefully ground up Paracetamol. Presumably quite tasteless in all the sugar and syrup – maybe even a weird kind of flavour-enhancer, who knows. Certainly Tooty didn't have a bad reaction to Paracetamol. I had seen her take a couple herself once, for what she called a migraine, that was plainly a hangover.

So, she wouldn't die from that, would she.

Yet, as I say, for me she was now deceased, and has stayed in that wonderful state. It's *what* you mean to do, not how you do it. Feeling the fulfilment and liberty of the true psychopath. Letting go. The *act*, not its substance. Or result.

She doesn't bother me at all now. I don't mind her ghost stealing my paper, pens and biscuits. Or the lover I might have had. I paid her out. I killed her. Let her rot, she's dead. And I'm free.

The Frost Watcher

*From an idea, title and scenario – and its accompanying artwork –
by John Kaiine.*

17

Every morning, Durdyn drove his father's flock of sheep up the slopes of the hills to a plateau under the mountains. Every sunset he drove them back down. By day the sunlight fell from strange skies like blue or white glass or golden smoke. Purple shadows, sinuous as water, flowed beneath the sheep as they grazed. But rain seldom fell. It was a hot climate for two seasons, and a cold climate for two seasons. Yet the cold was not often spiteful. It gave a little scratch, as a playful kitten might, not really meaning to hurt. The hot seasons, though, boomed across the land, brazen as a temple gong. Such things Durdyn inevitably was aware of, as he moved like clockwork up and down the terrain each day. And at night, the long cramped shackled nights of winter, the wet-fire nights of summer, that went sprawling through their tiny net of hours, *then* Durdyn dreamed. Princesses came to him at such times, spreading wide the rosy portals of their bodies. Or hill cats came, large as horses, and they ate him slowly, in a black triumph, praising him as they did so for the tasty gobbets of his flesh. (Only demons nibbled his soul. And they were everywhere. Mankind had fallen from the favour of the gods. The pleasures and horrors of the physical world were all that was left to men to sweeten and chide their psyches, and to make them forget all else. The demons alone reminded them of their utter spiritual loss.) The flock of sheep, originally one hundred and forty in number, had dwindled through the years. Durdyn had been given the task of herder when he was six. By the day he was sixteen, there were only twenty-nine sheep. And as for Durdyn himself, while he had grown in height and strength, becoming, at least in his own inner eye, a man, still he too had been regularly shorn, robbed of the coat of his true self. This he did not know. Yet, he knew. And knowing it unknowingly, in his seventeenth year, near evening Durdyn saw the Other One descending the mountain, walking down the slope through sun and shade, into the narrow, violet valley far below.

By the time the dusk began to come, the sheep were growing restive.

Some even ventured forward a short way onto the first of the lower slopes – but then turned back to the plateau, seeking guidance.

Durdyn had noted, absently, the bloody copper that infused their upper bodies as the sunset flared. The colour seemed to linger even when the sun had disappeared, having soaked into their wool. He had never noticed such a phenomenon before, but of course he had always, formerly, been driving them down to the valley by then, with no margin to spare for such things.

Now the stars were piercing through, and the Planet hardening after its daylight translucence. By this hour normally he would be below, just entering the village. Windows would be lighting, the gate of the sheepfold standing open, his mother there with the lamp to guide the flock home.

He had delayed to go down tonight.

Naturally he had. He had seen the *Other* go that way, and hung back. And next simply *hung* there, as if suspended from a dark nail stuck through the mountain air, he and the sheep.

The stars, however, returned him to responsible life.

He must get the flock off the hills at once. It would be tricky, too, in the dusk dimness, the constellations not fully bright, or the half moon yet risen. He was too big, thank gods, for his father to thrash him. But there would be the traditional tirade, a thrashing of the inside of his ears and brain – if not across his spine.

How foolish to have lingered. Could he even have imagined what he saw? (Durdyn knew he had not.) Very probably some old hermit, secreted as a rule in some upper cave, venturing out, crazy but irrelevant.

Durdyn began to gather the flock together. They were unnerved and unbiddable as sheep so often were.

His head was suddenly full – it had taken this long – of the ancient legends. How those figures had sometimes been noted, up there, high on the scarps of the mountains, their bodies fossilised by age and the wear of centuries to ebony skeletons, their faces leached back to smooth curves of bone, like polished white masks...

But *he* had never before seen one, nor did he know of any, man or woman, living, who ever had.

An antique story, a legend; that was what they were. Their purpose, established aeons ago by the gods, was utterly extinguished, for the gods no longer cared for Man, having grown tired of unrequited love.

As he had anticipated, it was difficult getting the flock down the night hills. In the valley soon he could spot the lights, and they seemed far off, farther than in reality they were. Up here, still, there was also a sort of light, luminescent and everywhere. He controlled the sheep with those commands and signals they were used to and, generally, obeyed. Above, among the glitter of stars, the cold Planet had begun dully to gleam. And...

Then.

It was an outcrop of pale grey rock by the track. He had seen and passed it many thousand times. Before, possibly, its textural similarity had struck him to the round textured 'O' of the Planet overhead. The likeness, that was, of two stones.

On top of the rock, against the luminous and separate grey of the sky, as if floating, weightless – yet mystically anchored – stood the Other.

Tall black bones, an ebony skeleton, a shape of perfect symmetry and grace. A face the cream-white of enamel, tarned with the deepest liquid-ink of eyes – nose, lips, jaw, lost in darkness – or gone – melted off... The figure was tented in a strawberry-coloured robe of incoherent patternings, drapes and apertures. These increased its effect of weightless drift – caught, motionless.

It had raised its thin left arm a little way. Across the murky sheen of coming night the arm extended, and the left hand, which might or might not possess a thumb and four fingers, was fixed in stark profile against the Planet's disc.

Within the robe a shift in the fabric, unseen but suddenly accomplished, gave out a deep and more somnolent red, as if the beating heart of this being had spilled a sombre scarlet flame.

Durdyn stumbled to a halt. All around him the sheep had clustered, half-aware, maybe, of a shadow that towered over them. Its gesture was like a fearful and beautiful, anomalous link that drew together the world and its creatures – with outer space. *Let me introduce you,* the stance of the being seemed to say, *to this mystery of cold grey stone.*

And then it spoke aloud.

It spoke in a voice not entirely unhuman, nor unlike the voice of a man.

"A Frost," said the voice, "is coming. A great Frost, greater than all frosts. An apocalypse of Frost. Be warned," said the voice, "of the coming of the Frost."

The voice ended. The left arm was lowered and the hand partly reversed, opening out. Durdyn did not take in the number of fingers. He saw only an ice-white burn scorched across the blackness of its palm, in shape like that of a terrible flower.

"The Frost is coming," said the voice again. "I have seen it."

Durdyn stood, himself speechless, unable to move. Instead the being moved, it swung about, its robe flaring up around it in a raw pink wing. And somehow it was off the rock, the track, gliding as if on runners along the slope of the hill, towards the edges of the mountains.

Durdyn could move again, and put back his head. The sheep too began to mill around. Vague as smoke, a crow fled over the surface of the sky.

The village was not as expected.

Something had overtaken and changed it.

All the lights burned everywhere, in every window it looked, and in most of the doorways too. There was a thick silence coupled, weirdly, with an intense sound. The silence was the nearer condition, a curtain, and beyond it the sound – or sounds, for they rose and fell like a blustering wind. They were apparently in the village square, the cause as yet out of sight, a gathering point of trampled earth, (the old temple to one side, and the well to the other), which for decades had pretended the village had some planning and importance.

As for the sheep-fold, no one stood by to assist Durdyn with the flock. The gate was shut and night's darkness, now fully down from top to bottom and here unlit, rendered the task more difficult.

Durdyn managed it, long practice making him able if not perfect.

When all the sheep were safely in and locked up snug, he turned his attention and his steps along the winding street.

Could the being, with his frost-seared palm, have caused all this? The lighted unoccupied dwellings, some with doors left wide, giving a vista of laid tables, the beer and bread waiting as if for invisible guests... Nobody was about. No, they were *all* of them from the sounds, in the square.

As Durdyn moved that way, cautiously, anxiously, he tried to decipher what the outcry meant. Was it alarm, or sheer terror? Or – as another bellow expanded – a kind of exaltation?

Not then, surely, because of the being's forecast of a great frost. That was a warning, ancient as the hills themselves, a part of legend: a story that might come to life, and had. For while the jilted gods had taken the miracles away, they had certainly left, as every year – month – day proved so well, the curses and catastrophes.

A huge light, larger than all the lamps together, bigger than *sunrise*, billowed up and raised the black ceiling of the sky.

Screams hurtled like spears. Animals screamed too. Dogs were howling like maddened wolves.

Durdyn found he had flung himself face down on the earthen street. But he did – could – not cover his eyes.

He twisted his head, glared into the scalded vault of the heavens. White-gold the radiance blazed, spangled with tiny flitterings of molten silver. It blinded and made him sick, his guts churning, as much from the light's physicality as from fear. And then, it died. The huge light went out, and for an instant left only a green visual aftershock.

When this faded at last, he beheld again the ordinary domestic lamps, still burning. The village had not been destroyed.

And incredibly, whisper to murmur to groan to shout, a thunder of human applause was starting to life now, in the hidden square.

Durdyn got to his feet.

He accepted he was not dead or blind, after all.

He wondered how many of the sheep-with-lamb might now miscarry when the cold months came, and how many of the hens cease to lay, and if the fruits would wither on the trees and vines and the beer sour in the vats, and the fish change to poison in the stream. He wondered if, whenever, if ever, he made a child on some wife as yet unwished for, it would come out a monster.

But the sky above was black. The moon had risen, a thickening shining slice. The stars glittered on. And the Planet hung as ever in the northern sky, pure and stony, the eternal dubious companion of the earth.

When he walked into the square, as he had thought, everybody was present. They were roaring and laughing and waving their arms. And some other men, in sleek uniforms that might have been to do with royalty from the Royal City in the south, or a city religion still of importance, were standing on the neglected parochial temple steps, smiling and acknowledging the crowd.

Dazzled, stunned, angry, nauseous, Durdyn discovered his burly father looming into proximity.

And now for the tirade, the ear-thrashing.

Bur Durdyn's father had not been aware of Durdyn's lapse. Durdyn's father laughed his sour beer-breath in the face of his son, and threw wide his ugly arms as if to embrace mankind.

"We shall be rich!" he blathered over the hubbub of hundreds of other hilarious and insane voices, his acid spit stinging in Durdyn's blistered eyes. "The village – *us*. Rich as bloody kings! The hub of all things we'll be, boy. The centre of this whole bloody world!"

7

While the months proceeded, the final warm days of the thirteenth-month year, and despite rising tides of excitement, village routines went on, mostly, as they always had. The fields were harvested and the fruits picked. Provisions were stored against the coming of the first of the two cold seasons. Animals were slaughtered and salted, dwellings mended and shored up. Everything now, however, was made easier and more effective by the influx of external help, some of it monetary, and much alchemific. The latter, of course, added to the general sense of elated optimism.

Early that winter, the village was renamed at a ceremony where four of the Royal City's princes presided. The new name was *Gate of the Sky*. This was a suitable recognition, it seemed, of the spot's supreme value and strategic relevance. For the area – the village – lay at the crucial axis of the alchemists' mathematical calculations. Out of the whole half of the world which held, day and night, always, a view of the Planet, *here* was the only appropriate place. And *from* here, maximum in capacity and exquisite alignment, they would therefore direct and expand the greatest phenomenon of Wonder the earth had *ever* seen: the Bridge of Light.

The Bridge of Light.

Gate of the Sky.

Life had changed forever.

In fact the erection, preparation and installation required many years. It must be flawless. Even the old golds had never attempted to hurry perfection.

Durdyn had been seventeen when the vast project began. As with other continuing routines, at first his also varied very little. He drove the sheep up the hills. Then drove them back down to the fold. He lived on with his loud father and loudish brothers, and their sullen mother, she always busy, always suppressing her angers – although in his childhood Durdyn, certainly, had borne the brunt of them when expressed. But things altered. Obviously they must. The village had been renamed and transmogrified, and was growing quickly into its revitalised skin.

In little leaps and bounds the place became larger. Extra buildings and roads spread over the countryside, to house and transport the community of alchemists, their assistants, servants, machines. Meanwhile domiciles at the village's centre were commandeered, paid for extravagantly, and improved out of all recognition. From a shopkeeper and owner of twenty-nine sheep, Durdyn's father morphed, with seamless glee, into the vulgar host of a flashy tavern, on the first new road made to open up the village to a teeming outer world. Within a couple more years, and another couple, he was wealthy in his own right, as the visiting masses endlessly gushed in. They came to view work upon the Bridge of Light, and dip their fingers, cloths and fine glass bottles in the Heaven Fountains of the Park of the Bridge, next to feast and drink at various hostelries. Some desired to live in the area as well, each in a fine house set with gardens and grounds. So architects and builders swelled the throng of guests at every inn.

By then, though, Durdyn had his own house, neither glamorous nor grand, but weather-proof and sufficient. The flock he had purchased from his father; the cash for this had been earned in mild mystified errands undertaken for the underlings of the Alchemia. (None of these jobs drew him anywhere near the Park, and once solvent he gave them up.) Despite his previous fear that any sheep-in-lamb would miscarry, none ever had. And there were again over a hundred of them when he took them on. That blinding light, that visual detonation of the first night, it went without saying, had been part of a display the alchemists had presented. It was a preview of things to come, and of the Bridge itself, that would fly outward, upward, and join the earth forever to the Planet of stone standing above. Heaven and Earth united.

Durdyn, too, was wed by the second year. Ejnas was a slim, dark girl, a beer-brewer's daughter. Durdyn had lusted for her briefly, and theirs was thought a suitable match. She did not seem to mind it for a short space of days, even quite to enjoy it. Then, abruptly, she assumed a passive, unimpressionable state, from which she produced with strange regularity, one child every year for three years. After which Durdyn and she slept together, literally that and nothing more. And like an invented three-time season, the recurrent children accordingly stopped. They were a pair of sons and a daughter. They looked like Ejnas, were slow and docile and uninterested, as she seemed to be.

Durdyn had expected not much. Not much had come to him. He still, often, if for a sort of recreation now, went into the hills with the sheep, and the two other shepherds he employed went with him.

He would sit, Durdyn, the other men at least a mile out of sight, gazing over the green-furred slopes, and beyond them, as beyond the blown-rose of the village that was swiftly a town, a near-city, with temples, mansions, an assortment of paved

squares and several parks. Right to the white tops of the
mountains he stared, at their cold double season crests of snow,
or, in the hot double season, crowns of ivory.

Not since the very start had Durdyn tried to ask if any other
had encountered the Watcher who descended to the valley on the
initial evening. Those he had spoken to ignored his tentative
enquiries. Or else laughed at and mocked him, and asked in turn
where he had got the strong drink that gave him visions of things
non-existent.

The Watchers were real only in myth. Creatures, perhaps
once partly human, that ascended to the highest levels of the
earth; and communed there either with the unforgiving elder
gods, or merely with the weather, day and night, time and
elements and sky, and space itself. True, in the legends, they *would*
watch, each of them, for some salient First: the first flower of the
warm months, the first raindrop after drought, the first snowflake
– and these, through some magical process, they would somehow
take the imprint of, and carry the shape and news of it to the
nearest human conglomeration. As for the ones who Watched for
frost, their task was to warn. For it seemed, in the long gone pasts
of the world, such frosts could destroy all – or almost all –
mortal, animal and vegetal life in the afflicted region. A warning
was meant to safeguard mankind, and receiving it men must
protect themselves, and what was theirs, the very best they could.

Yet no frost had come after the Watcher both descended to
the valley and returned from it, (by no other than Durdyn seen or
noted), the burnt silver imprint on that unearthly unhuman palm
less discounted – then simply *missed*.

Once, only once, Durdyn had told Ejnas how he had met
the Frost Watcher, poised on the grey flint wayside rock. The
being's mask-face, bone hand, that gesture, both beautiful and
fearsome, that seemed to beckon space and world together, and
introduced, as if never before had any witnessed it, the Planet of
cold grey stone, which rested, ever and always, in the upper
northern sky.

Ejnas herself had watched Durdyn as he talked of this. For that was what she did, not *look* at you, but *watch* you. And her manner of watching was not like that of the Watchers, real or otherwise. With her, it was as if, he thought, much later, you were some incomprehensible animal – or even *event*, some sort of *play* acted out in front of her. She had better attend, just in case. It might matter – oh, not in the scheme of things, or because she cared about it herself, but in the way one should check if a log might drop from the fire, or a pebble trip you up. Like that. Her – *their* – children were the same.

In the seventh year his father died – loudly, and very drunk – breaking his neck on the cellar steps, chasing after what he took to be a thief, but was in fact a nosy foreign customer. The inn went to the older sons, but a small share of the overall wealth to Durdyn.

Already he had done well from the sheep, currently six hundred of them. Ejnas bought herself the skilful making of three new gowns and some jewellery she fancied.

The funeral was a suitably miserable affair, followed by a jolly carouse. No one was particularly sorry to lose Durdyn's father. His wife, even so, would not marry again; she became and stayed a rich and wilful widow, having learnt her lesson the hard way. Durdyn thought Ejnas would not grieve for him, either, if and when he died. Nor would his children. He was twenty-four, however, and death did not seem especially pressing.

The town-city was huge by this date, or big enough for the villagers who had formerly lived in such a tiny warren. As for the project of the Bridge of Light, which even in the coldest of the cold seasons would draw hundreds, sometimes thousands of visitors, it dwarfed, both in fact and significance, all else.

From the beginning, the elegant and spacious acres of Heaven Park, hacked and pruned from surrounding country, enclosed it. Enormous trees, retained, or transplanted by novel biological alchemific methods, dominated the advancing avenues, all of which were lined with scented fountains and gracious statuary of marble, bronze and platinum. The paths themselves were floored with coloured mosaic, patterns and swirling reminiscent of avalanches and rivers in spate. Groves picturesquely opened on all sides, presenting ornate pools, and organised views of supreme attraction, and littered by eloquent-if-ambivalent shrines. After dark, soft alchemical lamps ignited, needing no apparent human agency, peacock and cobalt, cinnamon and blush.

At the start, the Park's core had comprised high walls, and curious obscuring screens that appeared to be formed solely of distorted air. But as time, six to seven years of it, whispered, ambled, flew and fluttered by, the most celestial shape amorphously began to grow visible, or at least detectable, through them. Like some gorgeous mirage seen under water or behind a semi-transparent veil...

A tower – was it? If it was, then at the lowest count ninety storeys high – higher – slender, yet weighty; solid as granite and iron, yet seeming nearly levitational. Physical, non-corporeal. Real. Mirage.

Persons who had seen, or thought they had seen it – remained bemused. Poets wrote fragments on its appearance and *presence,* employing such descriptions as 'gossamer steel'. Most agreed faint perfumes came from it, and sound – a musical yet tuneless, ever-repeating note.

In concrete terms, presumably it was the ultimate portal on which and from which the miraculous Bridge would both rest and rise, opening like a gigantic wing into the sky.

What everyone conceded, as from the beginning they had been told and thereafter shown, was that the edifice that lifted from the Park could bring nothing but prosperity and general good to the village-city of Gate of the Sky. They had and would prosper. They had and would be happy. They would be rich, rich as kings.

The Alchemia and its plan had brought all the world here,

and would continue to do so. These seven years on, see what had already been achieved. In seven more – how staggeringly enormous the city must grow to be, a metropolis whose magnitude not only rivalled that of the Royal City to the south, but which crushed the fame of any other, anywhere.

Durdyn did not think of this very much.

He only wondered, now and then, why he did *not* think of it, or if he ever did – forced to for a moment by the chat or speculation of others – his thoughts quickly strayed. As though running away very fast. Nor had he ever visited the Park.

No doubt, arriving late and unadvised of the first demonstration of the Great Plan, and petrified by the blast of light, he had been somewhat prejudiced against it all. And, even if he had dreamed or imagined the Frost Watcher, (he never, himself, credited this explanation), that too might have discoordinated his perceptions.

After all, ever since, had he also not benefited? Of course he had. House and wife and sheep and children, even the small post mortem share of his father's wealth, all of this had come to him through the preparation of the Bridge.

And it was not ugly, was it, either? It was mystical and marvellous. Artistic almost, you could say. A spiritual orgasm of beauty and aspiration, otherwise long-lost with the belief and trust in gods.

The years ambled and bolted by.

Durdyn, twenty-four years of age, often going up the slopes with his portion of the flock, on some nights of the hot months would stay there with them, all of them well-protected now by alchemific barriers from any large night-preying beasts. The sheep would graze, or lie down, feed their lambs in season, skip about if they wished. If able, as he did, they could stare at the wonder of the stars, those million miles of slowly, invisibly drifting brilliancies, flung up there so high in the dawn of time, skeins of jewels or shards of glass, or the tips of daggers, or nocturnal eyes. Perhaps.

Below, the burgeoned village-city had nothing to compare. The lights there were thick and greasy; even in the Heaven Park of the Bridge the lovely lamp colours sank with distance.

Durdyn anyway forgot the village-city really, when he was out of it. Nor did he recall frequently his wife, Ejnas, sleeping alone and, he supposed, glad to be so. He did not miss her.

But he, up here, had quite a different perspective. The earth beneath, the stars far away. Between them the mountains, and there the Planet, stone of a bone. Bone of a stone.

Gazing, he could sense himself come loose within his skin. His consciousness swam out of him to hang in air, suspended, and unattached to anything at all, not even to his abandoned flesh.

Inevitably maybe, it was during one such episode that Durdyn glimpsed, descending from the higher slopes, a dark, tall, bone-thin figure. It was not that of a shepherd. Could it be some visiting traveller who had journeyed on foot? Something in the shape, the way it moved forward and downward, the accompanying motion of what seemed to be its long robe, outlined only vaguely by the stars and crescent of a youthful moon – *something*.

Back into his body the consciousness of Durdyn fell, with a thump and shock that almost made him vomit. Not even recovered, nevertheless he flung himself to his feet, stumbling and almost going over, righting himself with a hoarse and hollow curse.

Rather before he was physically able then, he pelted across the hill, scattering the peaceful sheep. For Durdyn saw it was the Frost Watcher who was coming down again from the mountain tops and the sky. This could be no other. Durdyn had waited seven years for him, and not properly known he waited. But even his body knew now, running fleet as a mountain cat, and his heart banged like a drum to urge him on.

"Ah – no, *no*–" Durdyn cried. He stopped in his tracks, and the part of himself that not yet caught up with him collided home, and slumped across his brain.

Amazed, he felt boiling tears burst from his eyes. Covering his face with his hands, he stood there weeping. While the gaunt old man in the loose greyish garments also kept quite still, and looked at him.

"Who was it you expected?" the old man asked at length.

His voice was cool and oddly calming.

Durdyn's weeping lessened, ended.

For the first time in almost seven years, in almost all his adult life, he spoke his mind openly.

"The Frost Watcher. I thought you were that one, that being. Against the sky, over the slope, you seemed – you did seem – But no. Stupid."

The old man did not speak again for a little while. They merely waited there, separate and together, wound on the hillside in the deep weft of darkness, under the sparks of stars and silver claw of the moon. (In the north the Planet seemed only a scarred and worthless plate, a mistake left behind in the sky.) The sheep were settling like a moonlit cloud.

"My name is Crorth," said the old man finally. He had sat down on a boulder, which presumably had once usefully rolled here from the mountains to provide a seat. Durdyn did not know what to do. He did not want to go away, but could see no reason for remaining. He said, "The vill– the town is down there, a few more miles. Gate of the Sky. There are inns that will put you up, some quite cheap. Or charity houses, a few."

"You perceive I am poor," said Crorth.

"Yes," said Durdyn apologetically.

"And you think I must want to witness the City and the Heavenly Park, and the building yard where the Bridge of Light is being constructed."

Durdyn said nothing. What else did any stranger want who travelled to this place?

"Except," Crorth said, in his cool deep tones, a voice three or four decades younger than the rest of him would seem to be, "except the Watcher, the Watcher for the frost, came this way, as you have remembered well. How sorry I am," he gently said, "to disappoint you so cruelly. But you see, the Watcher will not return here. He came to give you his warning and he gave it. Only to you, since no other, even so quickly, was any more capable of discerning him, or understanding. But you at least were told, and you at least, poor boy, knew in your inner soul, the soul that the brain and body hide from themselves, and - where they can – from us. Yes, there in your deepest hidden awareness, you grasped precisely what the warning meant."

Durdyn gaped at the old man who called himself Crorth. He seemed to see Crorth more clearly with every second. The Watcher had been made of smooth white enamel and black bone; Crorth's form was of ancient cracked and smouldered wood. *Visible* eyes he did have, though. They were ink-black as the part-seen, unseen eyes of the Watcher had seemed to be. But these eyes were human in their own way.

"What did you mean?" Durdyn asked. "I *never* knew – I have *no* grasp of what it meant, or what I saw, or why I saw it – was it truly here? The Watcher?"

Crorth did not answer. His silence said: *What else? You knew. You know it all, as I've said.*

And Durdyn looked down at the earth and then upward at the dirty plate of the Planet. Durdyn heard himself, not Crorth, explain aloud that the Bridge of Light was to be a tactile ray of extraordinary Power. It would shoot full upward, not merely to cross space and to touch – but to *hit* the surface of the Planet. For then something would be caused to occur, some other condition would come to *be*. It was for this – this *occurrence* – that the alchemists, ever cunning, and thirsty always for new adventures, were aiming. Not a symbol, but a *happening*. And Durdyn thought, and pictured, and told aloud of a fist, sparkling and alight, *hammering* on a closed cold door of bone and stone.

Hammering.

"Why?" Durdyn asked, but not of Crorth now. "Not for beauty or pleasure, not to bring commerce and prosperity or happiness, or to unite the world with itself. Not even for a glorious entertainment. Not any of that. *That* is just the pretty jewel they've promised us. But the jewel is no jewel at all. It is — an *axe*." Durdyn said, "The Alchemia. They must always play. And when they do they break their toys carelessly, and human spines snap with them. The game's everything. Nothing else matters. The Bridge of Light is the hammering of a blazing fist on a shut door of stone. The Bridge of Light is the Frost the Watcher foresaw, and told me of. The Great Frost that may destroy everything."

Before the cold months came again to close the seventh year, Durdyn was every day climbing higher and higher up the hills. He had employed, well able to, a third sheep-herder, and left the sheep with him by daylight, and through the darkness.

Durdyn walked from sight along the slopes, then again upward. It was as if he must practice his ascending, improving it each morning, afternoon and evening, and throughout each night, always gaining higher ground, and then higher still.

In less than half a month he had regularly reached the footstools of the mountains, where huge rocks like dragon teeth thrust out. By the month's end he mounted the striated stairways of the lower peaks. He passed, under the waxing and swollen moon, lit sheer almost as sunrise, across the pale table-tops of vanished giants, through archways and fractured tunnels that rang with sliding waterfalls. Once having gained these regions, often of course he did not return below immediately. (He would frequently be gone from the City for some days and nights at a stretch.) He slept out on the mountains' bare carapace. The heart of the year was not yet spent. Nothing threatening came near him. He did not expect it would. He located Crorth's cave on the last day of that moon's waning crescent; thin as a wire both of them, the moon, the cave's entry. Crorth, too.

"I told you I'd come up and find you."

"Very well," said Crorth, as if they had been known to each other lifelong, and met as normal less than a day ago.

Crorth had told Durdyn of the cave simply when, on the night they *had* met, Durdyn had asked where Crorth might come from. Crorth was a hermit it seemed, no more, no less. He had vacated the ordinary world and its preoccupations in adolescence. Nothing had driven or lured him to do this; he had only gone away, as if it had been written out for him to do when he was at a certain age. As, say, other men felt the wisdom of learning a trade, making a marriage, or killing someone who had done them a mighty wrong. He had been at the cave some seventy years. Now and then he wandered out and off in various directions, journeys that might take him less than an hour, or more than two hundred hours. It seemed he had descended the slopes, to the area above the village-town-city, occasionally in the past. But he had never taken a vast deal of notice of its developments and enhancements. He had not concerned himself with the increase, not only in its size and scope, but in the alchemific functions apparent there, or a weirdness apparent there, that generally *would* be there in such spots favoured by advancement. That happened in recent history more and more, and in a large number of places. The seasons of the temporal world, however, like those of the climate, fattened and deflated in the same manner. Such altering things as had obsessed the village came – and *went*. One year nothing but a few huts, another year and a colossus dominated, twenty years from that moment and it was a ruin, or destroyed in some essential war. Or merely rundown and disintegrating, like a dying brick-and-mortar rose.

Why Crorth specifically went that way on the night Durdyn saw and ran to him, had no answer. It needed none, being (coincidence or fate) accomplished.

The cave was narrow inside, a corridor rather than a chamber. But a natural hollow provided a hearth by which Crorth sat, or slept, and where he cooked such food as he did not eat raw. In these activities Durdyn, having requested permission, and being told there was no reason not to, joined. (He brought food too, from his house, with wine and beer. These Crorth, invited, sampled, though he seemed to prefer his own pick of the wild roots, herbs, honey and water of the upper hills. In a short time, Durdyn felt he also preferred them. And then, having learned certain techniques, he too gathered such stuff and brought that as well as, or instead.)

If Crorth taught Durdyn, neither of them alluded to tutoring, teachers, pupils or lessons.

Crorth would talk in his finely-minted, elegant and expressive voice, and reply to any queries, if not always in a way instantly to be fathomed. For example, quite soon Durdyn surmised aloud that the Frost Watcher could dwell – if much further off, at some summit no doubt of the highest peaks – in a cave similar to Crorth's. No, Crorth mildly replied, it could not remotely resemble any such shelter. What then, could it be?

"Like the sky," said Crorth, "like the wind and the sun."

It was almost half another year before Durdyn, then below in the City for a short unavoidable spell to do with the business of his flocks, abruptly recognised the straightforward answer the riddle (which was not a riddle) suggested. The Watcher did not live inside any humanly-necessary home. Neither palace nor hovel, tent or cave. In the sheer openness of landscape, air, shadow and light such a being lived. That was all such a being would accept.

But a mass of information was given Durdyn during this period. Seamless yet multi-folded it draped him round. Surprising him with unusual contours and colours, depths and designs and hidden matters, whose very indecipherable textures were their *meaning*.

Durdyn had never loved any, woman, man or child. His father he had feared then hated and despised, his mother similarly. Ejnas he had wanted carnally but nothing else, and desire hurriedly starved from boredom. His children were like assets written in a ledger, which he tended to forget, unless he saw them, and even then he did not really welcome their significance in his life: they had none, nor he for them. But Crorth Durdyn did love, as he might have loved a kind and wise parent, or a woman that – not desiring her physically – still he was entirely fascinated by. Even a child, maybe, a son grown to excellent manhood and somehow much, much older than the father in knowledge, and profundity.

A crow flew down, at irregular intervals, to visit Crorth. It was solemn and black, with a small blanched patch beneath its right eye. It let Crorth feed it by hand, when he had anything it might like – a scrap of warmed seed-bread, a shred of the meat Durdyn had provided. Of Durdyn it took little notice, being neither wary of him nor rough. It had no name. Like the Watchers. They had no names, either. Just their title, their myth.

There came, about a year again since their first meeting, one deep night. Moonless, the stars were wrapped in the cloud of a changing weather, the heat once more draining off, the coolness breathing ever more deeply, readying itself to exhale snow and ice and the arriving cold. Crorth talked of the Watchers then. It seemed to Durdyn that Crorth's voice, like music, played on and on. And eventually Durdyn lilted down into sleep, still listening, still *hearing*, still cradled in what was said. So it was more recital than speech. As if Crorth, partly singing to him, offered a saga-poem out of the archives of centuries past. Though Durdyn, the next day, could not recall that Crorth, while he did this, revealed anything new, or more enlightening than Durdyn, (though perhaps in less lucid modes), had heard or read before.

They lived on the highest tops of the earth, the Watchers. They were, or there became, beings of black bone and white ivory. They ceased, if ever even partially they had been – to be human. They were elementals, spirits, creatures, dreams... Inexplicable, Eternal. Their purpose was to exist beyond all other life. And to *see*. And to *know*. And when unavoidable, they could go among Mankind, delivering their message, whether irrelevant or terrible. Their nature and their essence, and the reason for and of them, and their result, had been spilled off the world, because humanity no longer understood the language of the gods. Which men too, before the endless era of the Now, had once also spoken, and flawlessly.

During the cold season which followed, Durdyn was forced, by circumstance of climate and domestic issues, to remain in Gate of the Sky: snow buried the region; his children took sick with some ailment.

Concerned that Crorth might have difficulty too, Durdyn reminded himself that the hermit had survived as such already some sixty-nine years. Besides, Durdyn was trapped.

The snow covered the landscape in a second land of alabaster. This had its own geography. Obese white hills bulked up on humped white terraces and tiers, escarpments and perilous, white, unrecognisable overhangs. Ice had raised fortresses that any visitation of the frigid sun, a faint white-flaxen, caused to melt; opals must weep in such a way. Even the City, with its alchemific safeguards, experienced some problems with the traffic of wagons and carts and horses, while the management of estates, the potential perishing of vineyards, was crucial. A cruel season, the worst, apparently, in seven decades.

On a particular night, as Durdyn reviewed certain accounts to do with his flocks, Ejnas appeared, bringing him a – by then – unneeded flagon of hot wine.

He felt, as he usually did, that he must acknowledge her extreme goodness in doing any such thing. He thanked her warmly.

But Ejnas had fixed herself in the doorway, rather as the white snow had done in so many other free openings. Her dress was yellow, he judged, unless only the guttering lamplight made it so (the lights here were thick and greasy, even in the Heaven Park of the Bridge –)

"I know," she said, flatly, "you have a woman." (His mouth fell open: it had never occurred to him she might interpret his absences as something so trivial.) "It's no matter to me. I need no more children, though I will of course bear one, if you want. And men must be men. I know that from my father. But I would like," she added, in her soft, flat flute of a voice, "that you'd arrange a proper little settlement for us, myself and your heirs, in case ever you should want to go away."

Durdyn sat staring at her. He had never heard Ejnas make so long a speech. "But..." he said.

And she stood there like a badly-made doll, (only her face too stubborn and *lifeless* for a doll's) not speaking now, looking slightly over his shoulder. There was no point in denial. Instead, he thought, if he did not agree to her plan she would stick in her heels. Or poison him perhaps – he could somehow guess, maybe quite wrongly, that she would prefer to murder than to insist. However there was no reason he should argue, was there? He had no other he might need to arrange a pre-posthumous insurance for, while for a wife and children one should always make provision. Idly he decided it was feasible a hungry big cat might find him on the mountainside after the snow, and kill him for dinner. Or some sickness might claim him suddenly, up there. And, his body not being found, her rights could be disputed. (Or... here his thought paused... or, if he *did* go away... But where to? Why? When?)

Durdyn drew his scattered mental processes together and said to Ejnas quietly, "That is a very sensible idea. Thank you for suggesting it to me. Of course I'll do it."

She said nothing, only nodded. She would have, he supposed, to trust him to keep his word, at least for now. But he must not make her wait. Tomorrow he would seek a notary and the legality should be seen to.

In the morning, before even he breakfasted, Durdyn saw to this. The deed was drawn up, provision against his unspecified departure, signed and witnessed, and he took home a copy. Ejnas, who could not herself read, would get their elder son to read it to her. The boy, by now five years of age, had his letters. Durdyn had left her everything. She should be content with that.

The thaw began that morning too.

By noon enormous clods of snow, some larger than a cart, started to slide off from the roofs, falling in the streets with massive thuds, as loud as if the City were under fire by cannon.

That year, the hot season came a little early, as if to make up for the extremity of the snow.

Durdyn had tried, by then on several occasions, to find a reasonably safe and useable route whereby to reach the mountains and Crorth's cave. But it was never possible. And even as crystal hardness changed to slush, chunks of snow slipped and crashed savagely from the heights, as they had from the roofs of Gate of the Sky. The upper hills continued to be chancy for a while longer because of this. No sheep certainly were risked there.

But with the syrup heat of premature renewal the flocks returned, and Durdyn at last made his journey.

It had been many months by then. He wondered what he might find.

He saw the crow first.

It was out on the top ledges of the hills, among the stars of delinquent hot-weather flowers, a black blot hopping and pouncing through waves of vivid green and crimson and heaven-blue. It seemed to see and recognise Durdyn though, as he did it from the patch of pallor under its eye. Lifting in the air the bird flew straight up to him, brushing the top of his head gently with one wing. Never before had the crow deigned to greet him.

Durdyn laughed. "Are you well, old sir? You seem to be. And how is *he*?"

At which the crow merely soared away into the open sky. Something in its carelessness somehow reassured Durdyn. Foolish, no doubt. But about an hour after he reached Crorth's cave, and there Crorth was sitting on the handy rounded stone just outside, in the sunshine.

Crorth had not, unlike the crow, seen Durdyn yet. His relaxed stance, his closed eyes, might have convinced others he was sleeping. But Durdyn decided he was not. Often Crorth sat in this manner to think, or to listen. (Durdyn had once or twice seen people listen to a religious tract, or music, in such a way.) He had no moment's anxiety either that Crorth was dead. Nor was he.

As Durdyn drew near, Crorth opened his black clear eyes and lifted one hand.

"There you are," he said, smiling and unsurprised.

What else?

When he and Crorth met in the beginning, Crorth had released from Durdyn Durdyn's own subconscious awareness of hidden events to do with the Alchemia, and the Bridge of Light they meant to fashion. After that Crorth had, by whatever name one might call it – if any such name were needed – become Durdyn's teacher, as well as all the other roles he had, this old man, so oddly, and so kindly, filled. In doing this Crorth had not, of course, lessoned and reasoned Durdyn into an apathetic or cynical involvement, let alone acceptance of something unacceptable. What Crorth had accomplished was to take away *un*knowledge. Additionally Crorth, rather than sedate Durdyn's correct responses, had only disenflamed their frightened passion. Durdyn had known, and *knew,* the peril and the stupidity of an alchemific plan to *hammer* on the closed door of the Planet of stone. But he was no longer too terrified to comprehend.

Now as they sat together in the luxury of the sunshine, drinking a little beer, Durdyn told Crorth of the extra bustle there had been in the Village-City during the cold. And of how, despite the weather, visitors from the rest of the earth continued to pour into Gate of the Sky.

"Does this mean," Durdyn asked, "that the alchemists are

readying everything at last for the great Act they've promised themselves? Their peculiar tower-structure in the Park seems to be viewable now by anyone that cares to look."

"Have you?" asked Crorth.

"No. I – think I saw it in a dream. It was bigger, the tower, than any witnesses report."

He lifted his head and stared northward, and Crorth turned too, and gazed in that direction.

Over the grasses and flowers, above the ribcages of the mountains dappled by sun-flakes and all their own different marblings, the sky had nothing in it but for the Planet. In the rich sun of a fine afternoon, as ever, it was like a phantom. It might have been made from a single huge drop of dilute greyish milk, spilled on glass.

"What is up there?" asked Durdyn.

"I do not know," said Crorth. "But something surely is."

"In the oldest legends – oh, I heard them as a child now and then, and others speak of them now all over the town, as if they *play* with such ideas – the stories tell of fiery angels locked away inside the stone. Or icy demons. Or the old gods themselves, trapped by some fault – or else imprisoned there, to punish them... or monsters are encaged in the Planet. Or are the alchemists mining for dead souls, the rotted psyches of the dead? It's a prison, and the Bridge of Light will be the liberating axe. Or the key. Am I wrong? I thought you knew all things, Crorth. I thought you'd *know* what will be woken up there, and what it will do."

"It will wake, whatever it is. Or is not," said Crorth.

They passed the beer again between them.

"When?" asked Durdyn, after a long while had elapsed.

"I believe the Ceremony has to be," said Crorth, "in only another seven days. Then the Alchemia will shout. They'll call everyone together, with trumpets and fireworks, to see the wonder. And it will be done. And happen."

"Only seven," said Durdyn. He sighed. He said, "And you,

my Crorth, my father and mother, my lover and my son. What will *you* do?"

"Ah," said the old man softly. "Forgive me, dearest friend. I shall be gone."

Durdyn turned so fast the whole sky and landscape seemed to reel and tumble away. Even the Planet fell. Nothing counted or was believable save for Crorth, seated beside him.

But Durdyn was not as he had been, and already he knew what Crorth had actually said to him. "You mean, sir, you'll be dead."

"Yes, Durdyn. Quite soon. My body has told me, with vast tact and mildness. I have another place I must go to, and other things to do."

Durdyn wept, silent, and only for a short space. Crorth stayed quietly, as this went on, (as during the first occasion), and when it ended both men sat on in silence together, while birds flickered across the sky, and the warmth of the generous sun breathed down.

Not until well after midnight did Durdyn re-enter the village-town-City. He let himself into his house, discrete, and almost noiseless, not wanting to disturb, let alone summon any servant. And decidedly not his wife.

In that way he came up into the higher parts of the house, and heard, along a passage and behind a door, Ejnas howling in the delirium of sexual delight, while a man grunted a percussive accompaniment.

About two hours after, as he rested in the study below, the impedimenta of book-keeping spread about unperused – for the room was unlit – Durdyn noted his second shepherd go creeping by, and so out through the hindmost house door to which, it seemed, someone had given him a means of entry and exit.

Durdyn did not care, did not mind, was not alarmed or angry. It came to him that Ejnas and the second shepherd, now Durdyn had granted his wife a legal settlement to cover a mooted departure, might have some quicker move planned for her husband. (To murder *would* be preferable to her than insisting.)

But none of this carried any weight.

How could it, now?

No matter what plot or scheme, it was a leaf in the wind.

A single blowing feather.

1

The shout rose. Messengers of the Alchemia called it through the streets; signs of it were spelled out in beautiful coloured lamps.

It was to be the seventh day. The heavenly Park of the Bridge of Light. The venue had been fully prepared and was ready.

The final prelude, to which all were invited, being urged to come, would last for *only one hour* – miss none of it! The ultimate springing of the alchemific magic would last – *one second*. Only one. The process required no more. A single hour, a single second, that would thereafter linger and glow in the world's memory forever, flowing onward through the seas of history and time which followed, an inextinguishable torch to demonstrate the Power and Glory of the Human Race.

Ejnas dressed in a new gown. It was imported silk, and the hue of the ginger-spice travellers now brought regularly, from cities on the far side of the earth. She had a necklace of sea-pearls Durdyn had not given her, and which she had not told him she would like to buy.

The children were dressed also in their best, and seemed excited in their usual secretive monosyllabic way.

Ejnas did ask Durdyn if he would mind her, and the children, riding to the Park in the carriage of a woman friend: a contraption could be activated that would allow the party, when the vehicle was stationary, to get up on to the carriage roof and so have a better view of what went on.

He did not dissent. He was, of course, glad to be on his own.

Never had he tried to guess exactly what would happen. While to warn anyone would be pointless – as always it must have been. Perhaps, by this stage, to warn would be illegal, and punishable. (Or else, still, they would not even notice. A Frost Watcher had been unable to attract their attention after all.)

The seventh night was a night of gargantuan heat. The air bubbled, alcoholic with perfumes, incenses, the odours of cooked meat, and mortal flesh baking in its clothes. Overhead the stars looked huge and wet, brilliantly sweating too. The moon had risen early and gone down soon after sunset. As if it did not want to see what came next. Though even running to the world's other side would not, obviously, ensure sanctuary. It was already too late.

Durdyn had debated if he might himself not go to the Park, where he had never been, not once, since the whole preparation had begun. Then it seemed to him as futile *not* to go as to run and hide. An apocalypse must find everyone out. Better to remain, and meet the nightmare's eye as it unclosed.

He walked slowly and alone through the churning multitude that surged Parkwards. If any acquaintance hailed him, he did not notice. He glanced, as he went by, at familiar architectures, trees, lit windows. At a night bird perched on a roof, a cat on a balcony. Where, tomorrow, would they be, these innocent animals and buildings, views and symbols? None of them were culpable, none of *them* deserved whatever unleashed hell was coming.

Even, he thought a moment in sorrow of his three children. He should have smiled at them, stroked their heads, hugged the tiny girl. They learned their slyness and flatness from Ejnas, true, but other aspects which reduced them would have been inherited from him.

At least no other *knew* what approached. (That was best, as they were quite unable to combat or avoid it.) No other. Only he. He and Crorth, (Crorth, his only companion, who might already be dead.) And the Watcher. All and any Watchers. *They* would know. On the hottest night of the year, the white Frost would start to fall.

Having reached the Park, where the pretty lamps radiated from the sculpted trees, Durdyn climbed up beyond the statues and fountains to a massive stand that had been erected. It faced north, and outward naturally, towards the Park's central spot. Durdyn took care not to look at this until he had secured a place among the stand's upper tiers. Perhaps strangely, the structure was not packed with sightseers; the bulk of the crowd had gone inward to cluster about the centre, and be near the Tower, and so to the Event. They milled around down there, a seething multi-coloured earthquake of forms and gleams, and incredible rushes of noise and celebratory music. Trumpets *were* sounding, as Crorth had stated, and over and over showers of fireworks exploded in fractured zodiacs, whitish-pink, like flowers, or silver and golden as coins. Other entertainments also went on – jugglers and magicians did clever tricks, fortune-tellers told (presumably false) lucky futures. Dancers spiralled like maddened fireflies through the over-populated groves, to the clashing of metal discs and squealing of pipes.

Durdyn stepped up onto the highest tier, and then on to the bench there.

Now he would regard the Planet – and the Tower.

The Planet, focus of so much attention, was as ever: an opaque plate. Yet – how cruel tonight it appeared to Durdyn suddenly. Seated on its own highest stand in the sky, it waited to give back ill for ill, hate for hatred. All these centuries, and now revenge – but for what? What had any of them done to deserve from it retribution? *Lived*, Durdyn surmised. Lived as bestial and destructive human things. That would be enough.

But the Tower, that was another mystery. For a fact, even in the inchoate, half-visible state it retained, behind those shifting chemical veils that shielded it from the common gaze, he – or anyone – must still infallibly note it was extremely, maybe irrationally, tall. From the height and angle of his own elevated position, Durdyn measured the Tower. It seemed itself to hit against the apex of the night sky. It went up so very far it was, to look at, higher even than the planet. An ordinary optical illusion, yet unsettling. Compared to the Tower, despite its misty screening, the Planet became small and painfully easy to reach...

Durdyn after all seated himself on the bench.

He removed his attention from the Tower.

Yet now, though he stared again across the Park, at crowds, fireworks, beyond them all into the vistas of the City, the Tower stayed dominantly fixed on his inner eye.

He had seen paintings, brought here with all the rest of the foreign paraphernalia. They depicted a cornucopia of alien landscapes and buildings. And one of these had shown a *lighthouse*, a tower put up to blaze out a lantern, guiding ships that crossed the seas. This Tower resembled, Durdyn thought, that lighthouse. He could not quite think why. When the screens were removed, probably then he would understand.

The call to attention burst literally from thin air.

The trumpets blared once more, this time scores of them, deafening and startling the crowds. And then the stingingly loud voices that demanded, in a festive, loving, yet horrible way, complete silence.

Silence, obedient and servile, dropped at once.

Reluctantly, as if impelled by the unseen hands of Authority, Durdyn got to his feet.

In the blur of mechanical vocal reproduction, he absorbed the messages the voices now flung upon him, as on all those in the Park. And those everywhere? Durdyn believed the entire scene would be relayed through the astounding and incomprehensible sorcerous mirrors of alchemific technology that were rumoured to exist throughout the entire globe of the earth. Not a street, not an alley would miss, having access to such a mirror, an instant of this stupendous night. Even in slums, they would detect the booming, catch fleeting glints of the images. Even on the highest crags, in the deepest crannies, or balanced over the glass floors of oceans – somehow, somehow – nothing tonight could be avoided. Man would see. (The eagle would. The lion, the serpent, the fish, the ant. Unavoidable. Conclusive.)

And then the screens washed off from around the Tower.

Durdyn looked at it, and it seemed that he *had* been shown this before, in some dream, or a former era previous to his human birth.

A lighthouse. Assembled from coal-black pieces, that fitted together in the fashion of polished shards in a mosaic, or the scales of a lizard's back. Hard now, and unobscured, the Tower was the most concrete object present. All else had blended into the mist.

At the Tower's sky-touching top he made out, sidelong, the framework of a huge oval window. It would face full north. From there then, the beam would erupt. To fire the Bridge of Light.

They too were saying this now, the roaring voices. Almost one hour had gone by, apparently, since they had commenced the freeing of the Tower from its wrappings. And in another – what did they say? What? What? Another minute – one minute, only one – would come the single second, when some unseen and indecipherable means triggered and shot forth the shining arrow from the bow.

It was now. The time was now. All time was ending. All this would flame, and die.

The silence thundered once again and closed the world in a box of nothingness. Not even the grass moved. Not even a child cried. All momentum over, all crying done.

And then, the

Light-light-light-light-light-light-light –

As Durdyn walked up the hills, the sheep came trotting to him.

There was, to him, an aching sadness in this. They approached softly, but as friends and lovers might, as if to say farewell to him, for he must go away, and so must they also. He touched their shorn-prickle hot season backs, their soft-wooled heads. He caressed them tenderly as he had not, and maybe should have done, his unknown children. And content with his response, quiet as ghosts, soon they meandered from him again over the pastures.

He saw no shepherd. They were all below still; the Park, the City. But the protective barricades were active on the hills and the flock quite safe. At least, quite safe for a while. For the world had not been destroyed. Not yet.

Durdyn walked on under the moonless and star-blistered night. So high, so far, he could still, if he wished, behold the pathway of the awful conflagration of the Bridge. But it was not omnipresent here. And sometimes, among trees or behind the outcrops of the enduring rock, it could not be seen at all. Nevertheless, its shadow fell, the new-invented shadow cast by the Light. How black the shadow, and how *lightless*. As shadows are.

Overhead, the stars changed position slowly, while Durdyn slowly climbed, upward, upward. Through the leaden anticlimax of horror deferred.

He did not go towards Crorth's cave, not now, that was finished. Like the rest. Upwards.

Upwards, beyond the last stands of the trees, into the higher air, much cooler and ringing with unheard notes. Should he glance back, he could see very well the Bridge again, and the Planet. Some had speculated in the last days prior to the unleashing of the Light, that its journey to contact the Planet must take at least some further days. But this depended on the old argument that wise men had debated before, as to whether the Planet lay out actually in the far environ of Space itself or, no 'planet' at all, simply adjacent and on top of the uppermost atmospheres of the earth.

Durdyn did not know, and did not bother with it. Nor did he turn to see the Bridge. (Though now and then its relentless shadow slanted across or before him, would not be completely shut out.) It had seemed to him, however, below in the Park, that the ultimate finger of the fiery flight *had*, in the one second, touched already the deadly face of stone above. And *at* the contact, even if all things did not – as he had thought they might – disintegrate, still a sort of pallid glimmering began on the Planet's surface, like an ember waking, but seen dimly, through a darkened glass.

Upward, Durdyn climbed.

Lands of stone also, visually cold grey in the hereabouts diminishing heart of the season, torn and carved, polished and roughened. The white bone peaks filled the night ahead. Ignore the shadows. That vague shifty sheen – there – there – might not be the reflection of any Light at all. An illusion, or delusion, or some curious internal lamp...

Upward. Horror deferred. Yet still...

To come.

There was nowhere else on Earth for Durdyn, now, to go.

The light had sprung from the Lighthouse as a tiger would spring, outward and forward, faster than... light. The ray was like a blinding moonrise, but even as it streamed and widened, it grew icier and more crystalline, hardening to white diamond. Fastened inside the adamantine envelope, colours then began to be created, luminous, sinuous, but changing with each split of the splintered single second. Fiercer and *sharper* they became, piercing to an agonised register of sight. And any that had eyes could see. It was a rainbow, the Bridge. But every tonal chord of it struggled savagely to and from position – sea waves, lava–a *fight*–a battle–

> the bloodied ruby reds shattering and shattered
> by burnt ambers that rushed
> crushing to obstruct the poisoned poisoning
> of lemon citrines to flindered topaz where
> these locked in combat
> on green scalded peridots which stabbed

deep drowning emeralds whose clawing bite
strangled with wild searing strands
smashed turquoise as they trampled on
the spears of shivered aquamarine
whipping the bruised shoaled indigo
of sapphires whose vampire lust
gnawed at pitiless amethysts while they in turn
spun bladed webs more darkly pale
than purple
death forgetting
wounds

– surging
sparkling, metamorphosis – eruption like orgasmic war – the inspiration to enlightenment or sheer madness.

A billion seething flakes flew off from this detonation, next flittering down from far above to land, with ironic leniency, on the multitudes beneath.

The people had assembled for a civic festival. The slowest of them currently grasped this which happened was no such average thing.

Whatever and whoever they were, a vast amount of them beheld visions in the dazzling turmoil of the ignited Bridge of Light.

Angels, they saw, some of them, twenty or thirty feet tall, with sky-spanning wings of flame. Or demons as tall or taller, clad and shod in clotted icicles. Or gods – so tall, these, their high-up heads were not to be spotted, but they were robed in tempests, gales, winds and lightnings. Some saw monsters and could not describe them, so foul, so unspeakable they must go unrecalled. Or souls, perhaps, some saw even those. Lost souls. Or merely memories. And some members of the crowd collapsed, fainting, or in fits. Some were rendered temporarily without sight. Some did, for a fact, become for a brief while lunatics. Others succumbed to uncontrollable mirth, or sobbed.

Battalions coupled on the lawns or in the fountains, or leaning on the trees in the maelstrom of the multi-coloured Chaos. Some – not a great number these – fled, or attempted to, the gathering being sufficiently large and impacted that most activities were rather awkward, but flight the most. Very few, given the amount of persons present (or viewing elsewhere) died, either then, or shortly afterwards. It was surprising, this, they said. But a little later on they said it was surprising *any* had died, except of course from extreme stimulation or insupportable joy. For the Bridge was the wonder of the world, and would bring only beneficence. By day gleaming ethereally and by night in splendour, it was a signal purely of the marvellous genius of Mankind, and of miraculous additional events to come. Only good *could* come of it, or its contact with the Planet, from the touching of whose stone casket nothing but blessing might result. To wait, and to believe, that was all Humanity need do. (All that had been left it, the solitary option.)   But for how long a space could they indulge themselves in this blindfold hope? How many years – months – days – in the name of the forgotten gods, remained? Before the Hammering of the Light was answered, the axe broke through, the key turned – before the sky fell and the world ended?

Upward he walks, the young man whose name has been Durdyn, upward, upward. (Tomorrow the crow will find him. It will ride on his shoulder, and soar across the moon for him, and fill chosen minutes for him with antic intriguement and laughter, or the pleasant familiarity that close companionship may bring. But that is tomorrow. Tonight he will be alone.)

He has left the heat and the Light behind him, in the valleys and on the lower hills, and here the faces of the mountains confront him with their incompleteness of enamel features, which are like those of the Watchers, just as, where visible, the thin strong bones of the mountains are ebony. Watchers climb upward. They attain and stand on the upper places, the mountain tops, and *watch* there for the first raindrop, first flake of snow, petal of first flower, scar of first great frost. And there they fossilise as the mountains do, to skeleton and mask, with tarn-black eyes, and the dissociate beauty of all living yet unhuman creatures. He that was Durdyn ascends the mountains. He is to be a Watcher. It is not a decision or a choice. A fact, that is all. But as he climbs (upward, upward, upward) his thoughts are still partly those of a man, if, with each step, that man slips farther off from him, as do the lowlands and the City and the Bridge, and the earth.

What then did *he* see when the Light began? A devil? A god? Something it was, because he turned from it in some clear – yet unreadable – way , if quite serenely, and next quietly moved down through the stampeding of the crowd, gaining the outer streets and presently the countryside beyond Gate of the Sky, with an adept unhindered quickness that is astonishing, do you think? What was it, therefore – an angel? For a moment Durdyn had believed it was. But then, that Being he was to become, *that* saw, and so Durdyn did also. Not an angel. Instead a line of Others, figures of bone and mask, robed in folds, patternings, apertures – Watchers – *Watchers*, positioned all along the burning Bridge, at intervals, away, away into distance and invisibility, motionless, mute, inimical. It was not that they were there physically, not then. But that they would *come* to be. In the future. When that future dawned. If they were guardians, or sentries posted for protection, who could say? Or if they had *any* purpose. Or if the purpose was ever to be revealed. And besides – they melted, and were gone. And then the angel did appear. But rather than an angel, it was a big white moth, which flew abruptly against and into the core of the Light-rioting rainbow of the heavenly Bridge. For another single second then, one more needle-point of time, it poised, the moth, its own unspoiled whiteness shining in the Light's fire – and then it too expanded in blissful flame, spangling more brightly, it seemed, than anything ever had; even the Bridge, maybe, even that. And after this the moth sizzled out, extinguished, a sooty spark that gave no longer any light at all, and was dull dust before it met the ground.

About the Author

Tanith Lee was born in 1947, in North London. Being dyslectic, she didn't learn to read until nearly 8 years old. By 9 she was writing. Early jobs encompassed library and shop work, waitressing and clerking. In none of which she was a shining star. At 18, however, she still managed to write the 1st draught (around 1,000 pages) of what became her early novel *The Storm Lord*. In 1974 DAW Books of America accepted this (by then re-written) novel plus *The Birthgrave* and *Don't Bite the Sun*. Which launched Lee on her true life – that of a professional writer. Since then, she has published around 92 novels and collections, and written for BBC radio and TV. Her work has been translated into over twenty languages, including Russian.

Lee writes in many styles – and genres, e.g.: Fantasy, SF, Contemporary, Horror, Detective, Historical, YA and Children's Fiction. (Also some poetry, which she refers to as Catterel – as opposed to doggerel.) She has won several prizes, not least the August Derleth Award, and the World Fantasy Award (twice), and was also honored by the title Grand Master of Horror in 2009. In 2013 she received a Lifetime Achievement Award at World Fantasycon in Brighton, England, just down the coast from her beloved home.

In 1992, she married the writer-artist John Kaiine. They live on the Sussex Weald, under the Iron Paw of 2 black and white cats.

LEGENDS

Stories in Honour of
David Gemmell

David Gemmell, who passed away in 2006, left behind a legacy of memorable characters, epic settings, and thrilling tales. In 2008, a group of fellow writers and friends led by Deborah J Miller and Stan Nicholls founded the David Gemmell Legend Award in his honour. In 2013, a group of today's fantasy writers have set out to produce a book that honours the memory of a man whose work has so inspired them. Welcome to the land of Legends…

Featuring original stories from:

Joe Abercrombie, Tanith Lee, James Barclay, Stan Nicholls, Storm Constantine, Adrian Tchaikovsky, Juliet E McKenna, Jonathan Green, Gaie Sebold, Jan Siegel, Anne Nicholls, Sandra Unerman and **Ian Whates.**

Available as a paperback, an e-book, and a numbered hardback edition signed by all the authors, limited to just 150 copies.

Lightning Source UK Ltd.
Milton Keynes UK
UKOW05f2352211013

219515UK00004B/502/P